"REACH FOR THE SKY!"

Slocum quickly looked around for a place to escape, but he knew he was under the threat of three revolvers—and even bad shots wouldn't miss at that close range. Slowly, he raised his hands as the one on the sorrel rode in and took his pistol.

The bandits wore flour sacks over their heads and linen dusters to hide their clothing. One rode a bay with scars on his right front leg; another was aboard a well-muscled paint. He wouldn't forget their mounts.

"Damn nice horse you got there—" the leader said. Then the lights went out, and Slocum didn't recall anything but the acrid taste in his mouth . . .

DON'T MISS THESE
ALL-ACTION WESTERN SERIES
FROM THE BERKLEY PUBLISHING GROUP

THE GUNSMITH by J. R. Roberts
Clint Adams was a legend among lawmen, outlaws, and ladies.
They called him . . . the Gunsmith.

LONGARM by Tabor Evans
The popular long-running series about U.S. Deputy Marshal
Long—his life, his loves, his fight for justice.

SLOCUM by Jake Logan
Today's longest-running action Western. John Slocum rides a
deadly trail of hot blood and cold steel.

BUSHWHACKERS by B. J. Lanagan
An all-new series by the creators of Longarm! The rousing adventures
of the most brutal gang of cutthroats ever assembled—Quantrill's
Raiders.

JAKE LOGAN

SLOCUM AND DOC HOLLIDAY

J

JOVE BOOKS, NEW YORK

SLOCUM AND DOC HOLLIDAY

A Jove Book / published by arrangement with
the author

PRINTING HISTORY
Jove edition / August 1997

The Putnam Berkley World Wide Web site address is
http://www.berkley.com

ISBN: 0-515-12131-2

PRINTED IN THE UNITED STATES OF AMERICA

10 9 8 7 6 5 4 3 2 1

1

April 1, 1881, Tombstone, Arizona Territory

The stage driver's loud "Whoa!" hauled the two teams of lathered horses to a halt before the stage office. A cloud of dust swept over them and finished frosting the passengers' clothing. The jingle of harnesses and prancing hooves of the hard-run animals was mixed with the metallic rasp of the cogs on the brake pedal as the operator locked it in place above them. Slocum saw the freckled-faced youth rush out of the office to open the coach door as the four male passengers waited for Mrs. McClain to exit first.

Her expensive blue-velvet dress was floured from the road dust churned up by iron rims and horseshoes. Still, the tall, willowy woman under the large ostrich-feathered hat lost none of her regal bearing as she accepted the boy's hand and then stepped delicately down on the boardwalk. Her face looked chiseled from white marble, and her blue eyes were as deep as any ocean, matching her dress. Hair the color of ripe Kansas wheat was piled under the hat. She looked up and down the street as if expecting to see someone there for her. Slocum guessed her age as close to thirty, but she had the figure of a girl in her teens. Certainly not the usual sort of female who descended the stage steps into this hellhole.

Slocum, grateful to be free of the cramped coach, stretched his six-foot frame. Then he took his saddle from the driver, who handed it down from the coach's roof, and set it down on the horn while he waited for his canvas war bag. He heard the woman ask the youth if he had seen her husband. The boy shook his head, and then directed the two Mexican employees to walk the lathered teams until they cooled "like Moses Larkin had told you to do with them!"

The two Latinos said something in Spanish, and went off leading the worked-up animals, who pranced and danced on them. For a moment, Slocum wondered if short men could handle the horses, but the Mexicans proved capable, and soon were circling back and forth in the short half block of street with their charges beginning to slow down and doing less rearing, coughing, and snorting.

He needed a saddle horse for himself, and knew that the OK Corral was only a block away down Allen Street on the right. He lifted the saddle to his shoulder, the fenders, stirrups, and girth slapping him. Then he hefted his war bag in his other hand, and when he straightened, came face-to-face with Mrs. McClain.

"Your husband has been detained?" he asked.

"I'm certain Landon will be here any moment. I had written and told him of my arrival. But thanks for your concern, Mr. Slocum."

"There's a very respectable place down the street. Nellie Cashman's. It is the only place I know of in this town for a real lady to go into. It's a famous cafe and hotel, if you should need a place for the night."

"Thanks, but I am certain Landon will be here any time now."

"Yes, ma'am." He started down the boardwalk. His boot heels clunked on the hollow wood as he strode to the corner and went west on Allen Street for the high solid board gates under the OK Corral sign. Forced to shift his load from his shoulder, he ducked entering the man-sized door cut in the closure, holding the saddle before him, and once inside, piled it all on the ground in the deep shadows of the compound.

He spotted a man, hatless, in a white shirt with red garters on the sleeves, pitching hay to a pen of grateful horses. They stirred around, some threatening to kick and bite each other until their social order was settled. The man only nodded to acknowledge Slocum's presence until he finished the hay feeding. Then he dragged out a kerchief and mopped his sweaty face.

"Hot as hell, ain't it?" He drove the fork into a pile of hay and turned, shaking his head.

"Warm," Slocum agreed.

"Name's Curt Taylor. What do you need?"

"A saddle horse."

"All you Texans must have sold your mounts and come out here. I can tell you I haven't got a damn thing you'd want. You are a Texan, aren't you?"

"I've been there," Slocum said, not anxious to advertise himself as a son of the Lone Star state.

"You're a cowboy by the cut of your clothes anyway. Damn, these miners will buy anything has a head and tail on it. You cowboys are all alike wanting a good horse. I can't find enough of those kind to sell."

"Maybe I should be in the horse business?"

"You bring me some good surefooted cow ponies and I'll pay a hundred bucks a head for them."

"Where are the ones that you have for sale?"

"Over in that shed, but you won't want one," Taylor said, shaking his head as they started across the yard.

Slocum looked down the line of animals. The big-headed black on the end was a single-footer, not an animal he wanted to take out through the prickly pear. Next to him was a bay with splints on his shins that would be crippled in an hour. Then a fat-butted Appaloosa who drew up his left hoof to cow-kick at anyone who thought they'd move him over. He was too short-backed to ride comfortably, not to mention his sour disposition, and the rest in the line were in worse shape. Slocum sighed and looked back at Taylor. Nothing there would get him two miles down the road, let alone to the Dragoon Mountains.

"Where can I get a decent saddle horse?"

"There ain't none in this town. I could have bet you wouldn't have bought any of these. My competitors haven't got anything better. Every miner wants to ride to some distant claim. You can't keep enough horses for them to ride, let alone a horse like you want."

"Surely someone has some good horses." He stopped beside his gear ready to leave, disappointed at the prospects of walking the twenty miles out to the Lady Luck Mine.

"If you can get one off the Earps, the Lowery boys, or Old Man Clanton's bunch." Taylor laughed. "They've got them, but they won't be cheap."

"How much?"

"Hell, I don't know. Too much, I imagine."

"Thanks." Slocum swept up his gear to leave.

"Yeah, good luck. Maybe you can win one in a poker game," Taylor shouted after him, then chuckled at his notion as Slocum exited the gate.

The sun was sinking behind the purple Whetstone Mountains in the distance. He might just as well find a place to bunk. Besides, his belly was trying to gather in his spine and he wanted a good meal before he planted himself down for the night.

At the corner of Third Street, he looked toward the stage office and saw the figure in the blue dress seated on the bench and looking forlorn. He decided to check on her, out of respect for an honest woman stranded in a tough place. It would be dark soon. Where was her husband?

"He hasn't made it?" Slocum asked as he came up to her.

"No," she said, as if startled at his return.

"Might I suggest that you join me for some good food at Nellie's?"

"Oh, no, thank you."

"Mrs. McClain, I'm certain your husband has been detained by something unavoidable. He would not expect you to sit here and starve while he hurries to join you."

"But what if he came?"

"I am sure the young man inside would direct him to Nellie's cafe."

"This is highly unusual. I mean, I hardly know you, sir. Where I come from in Chicago, it would be considered in poor taste for me to do this." The frown on her smooth forehead was enough to warn him of her concern about the etiquette of such an arrangement.

"Mrs. McClain, in Tombstone it would not be any such thing, just good manners and a pleasure for a saddle tramp to have your company at a meal table with me."

She looked to the heavens for help and wrung her hands. Then she swallowed hard as if she had made up her mind at last. With resolve she bolted to her feet before him.

"I guess if we can ride side by side in a coach, then surely in good faith, we can face each other across a public table. Besides, I am very hungry. Strange, but I think perhaps a good meal might settle me."

"I won't bite either," Slocum said, with a small smile for her as she lifted her skirts and went inside to tell the boy her plans.

The boy agreed to send her husband on to Cashman's if he came for her while they were gone, and then nodded for Slocum to stow his gear there until he came back.

They started down Allen, the flames of the sun set bathing the street in a red gold river flooded with riders and rigs. The strong aroma of cigar smoke and booze drifted out of the bat-wing doors of the saloons that they passed. Sounds of tinny piano music carried on the evening wind. Occasionally the raucous wild scream or laughter of a whore challenged them, along with the click of roulette wheels with winners shouting and losers groaning as Tombstone came awake from a sleepy day.

Men fresh from dusty hells underground or above the ground were crowding the boardwalk in pursuit of something to wash the grit from their throats. At the approach of Slocum and Mrs. McClain, the men parted and touched their filthy headgear for her. They were men that would give a year's pay to sit and talk for an hour with such a beauty. They too admired her long hips and firm derriere. Some even undressed her with their eyes in passing until Slocum guided her away from their gazes and on toward Fourth Street.

But nary a stray derogatory word was issued aloud about her presence among them, nor was anything out of line uttered within her hearing. There was nothing more than elaborate bowing in her path and the doffing of hats to "Ma'am." The strict code of miners regarding an honest women was unwritten, but it carried a swift death penalty to the infidel who dared break the rules. Slocum understood that as they left the street and entered the cafe.

"You know her? This Nellie Cashman?" Mrs. McClain hissed.

"No, but I've eaten her food when she had a place in Tucson and I know her reputation."

"Oh," she said as the Chinese waiter led them through the tables of customers. He held the seat for her, then handed them both menus.

Slocum soon discovered that, with her back to the door, she would surely swivel her head off trying to see who entered the place. There was no way she could ever eat without turning at every rattle behind her to see if her husband had arrived.

"Here, let us change seats. So you may watch the entrance," he added to settle her wide-eyed look of shock.

"I look that upset?"

"I understand your concern," he said, and they switched chairs.

She dropped into silence and fidgeted with her hands on the table, then in her lap, then on top again. He wanted to reach over and settle them. The poor man was coming, no doubt, and worrying would do nothing to hurry him.

"You may order for me," she said, then dropped her gaze to the tablecloth.

He knew how to do that. What was this lovely angel doing in Tombstone anyway?

"Our ranch is in the Swisshelm Mountains," she said, straightening the napkin in her lap.

"Oh."

"Have you ever been there?" she asked.

"I've been by them," he said, not anxious to tell her he had been with the U.S. Army chasing renegade Apaches when they went past the range.

"Are they beautiful?" she asked.

"The mountains? Oh, yes."

"You see, I know nothing about ranching," she said with a pained look.

"Oh, you'll catch on quickly," he said as the waiter returned. Slocum ordered steaks, roasted potatoes, and coffee for them.

"I hope so." She sighed and dropped her gaze into her lap again.

There was little he could say to reassure her that things would work out. He didn't know her man nor anything about him and his ranching operation. Surely he would at least arrive by morning, or at least send word to her by then.

"Landon is building up the numbers of cattle on our place."

"He's working hard then. I bet you'll like it."

Their water glasses and steaming coffee came. Soon the rich-smelling food arrived. Slocum hoped it would allay some of the tenseness between them. He busied himself cutting on his steak and wondering how a woman from an obviously well-to-do family had married a man who ranched in the Swisshelm Mountains. There was more to the story than he knew, he realized as he sliced the tender meat and then tasted the first bite. As good as Nellie's fare had been in Tucson a few years before, this was even better. He took his cup of coffee in his hand and blew the steam away while studying the attractive woman across from him. She ate delicately.

"You were right, I suspect this is the best food I've had since leaving Chicago," she finally said, looking up at him.

"Would you do me one more favor?" he asked. Might as well get it out before they went any further.

"What is that?" She blinked her thick lashes at him as if in a quandary over what she should do next.

"Nothing personal," he said with a smile. "But this is a very tough town. Please take a room in the hotel here. In the morning, I am sure your husband will be here for you."

"Stay here?" She looked rather distressed at his request.

"Yes, this is the fortress you need to stay in."

"Fortress?" Her blue eyes blinked at him in a lost way, questioning him.

"Your husband would want you to do that if he was here."

"I shall do as you wish," she said obediently, and then busied herself with her food.

He felt better. At least she would be safe for the night. That issue resolved, he could turn his attention to the Lucky Lady Mine in the Dragoons. He'd paid for a fifty-foot shaft to be bored on the site, and he needed to see what they had found. He had other things to do too, like getting current assay reports on the new ore. He had all his money invested in this operation and it needed to be successful.

Still, he faced the need to find something to ride up there. Otherwise the war would be lost for the lack of a horse. But no good horses were for sale. As he looked across the table at the angelic form in the chair opposite him, something niggled at him. There was something not quite right about the situation, and it kept coming back to where her husband was. There had to be something very wrong, or else the man would surely be there—no one left a woman as beautiful as her waiting.

2

"Gawdamnit, where did that son of bitch go?" The man brandishing the revolver was unsteady on his boot heels as he held open one side of the bat-wing doors of the Oriental Saloon. Dressed in a black frock coat and hatless, with his blond hair combed back, he wore a pallor of death on his hollow face in the light flooding out of the saloon.

"Who are you after?" Slocum asked, turning to see what the man was looking at in the inky night.

"That son of a bitch." He blinked his eyes as if wondering why Slocum had stopped when everyone else had run for cover at the first sight of him waving his six-gun around. "You must be new in these parts, sah?"

"Slocum's my name."

"Holliday's mine," he said, as if pleased to meet Slocum, and then holstered the gun. "Son of a bitch tried to cheat me at cards. Ain't a man alive, drunk or sober, can cheat on me, Slocum."

"I've heard that said before."

"The hell you have? Enter this decrepit hellhole and I shall buy you one good drink. Then you can fend for yourself, sah."

"I'd consider it a downright honor to sip some of your private brand."

"Private brand, ha!" Holliday held open the swinging door for him to enter. "I drink the best they got in here and let me warn you, that ain't much. Where have we meet before?" He waved the bartender over and held up two fingers, then turned back to lean against the bar and study Slocum up and down.

"Where in the hell have we met before, Slocum?" Holliday asked again as he looked at him as if considering some past event.

"Queen of the cow towns." Slocum put his elbows on the mahogany bar, tipped his hat back, then leaned forward and examined the voluptuous nude picture on the wall.

"Dodge. Sweet Jesus, she was the cradle of the civilization in her day. Damn, they never stuck Adam and Eve in a better place than Dodge City when the cattle were rolling in and the trains full of them bellowing devils left four times a day." Then his speech was broken off by phlegm in his throat, and he bowed over and began coughing into a fresh white kerchief. It was not the cough of smokers, nor one caused by trail dust. Slocum realized that Holliday was in the death grip consumption.

Finally, recovered but teary-eyed, Holliday downed the first jigger of whiskey set on the bar. Then he wagged his head for time to regain his composure, then straightened and slapped his palm on the bar.

"I still can't recall you, but no doubt it will come to me," he finally managed in a civilized fashion.

"No doubt." Slocum motioned for the barkeep to bring him the cigar jar. He removed two long-leaf tubes, then scented their length and nodded in approval that he would take them. He slapped down the twenty cents on the bar. Holliday refused his offer of one, so Slocum put the spare in his inside coat pocket. Under the bar, he scratched a lucifer to life, and ignited his own.

His elbows supporting him, his back to the bar, Holliday gazed around the busy room. There were plenty of card and roulette games in the cloud of smoke that hung like a fog in the bottoms on a fall Alabama morning. Obviously Holliday was well in the chips. Slocum was pleased his presence had humored the man, for the opposite occurred more frequently.

"What business have you got here?" Holliday asked.

"A mine, up in the Dragoons."

"You're a dreamer, huh, like that darned Wyatt Earp?"

"I guess," Slocum said, not overly pleased to be linked to the white-shirted bastard. He waved the bartender over to refill their glasses.

"Gawdamn, that son of a bitch Wyatt spends his every waking hour looking for a good strike." Holliday's head wobbled on his shoulders. "There ain't none left. Ed Sheflein found the best one and sold the son-a-bitch. Smart man."

"There's got to be another," Slocum said.

"Hell." Holliday held the brown liquor in the jigger close to his own face. "There's always more whiskey, more whores, more stiff pricks, but there ain't but one good strike to a place like this, sah. See—we're all like those little pigs at a sow's belly, sucking on her tits. There ain't enough for everyone comes along, is there?"

"You have a point, sir."

"You were there at Dodge, Slocum. What the hell did you do with your money?" Doc twisted around and leaned on the bar to stare in the mirror. "You spent it like the rest of us damn fools did. Just like us, easy come, easy go. It was going to last forever, wasn't it?"

Slocum nodded beside him, then tossed down his glass.

"Back then, there was never going to be another bad day, was there, sah?" Holliday said.

"That's right."

"I'll buy this round," Doc said, slurring his words more than before. He waved the barkeep over for refills.

"I like an intellectual men to talk with. Someone by Gawd that don't look blank at me over a few five-dollar words. You know what I mean?"

"I understand perfectly."

"You want a woman tonight?" Doc asked, lowering his voice.

"No. Worse than that, I need to buy or rent a good horse to ride up and check on my claim."

"Well, don't go to the stables. Oh, Jesus, they don't have anything worth a shit. A hundred-million-dollar silver strike—hell, more than that—and there isn't a horse worth a tinker's damn in the whole place for sale."

"Where do I find one?"

"I don't know." Holliday put his arm out straight and braced himself on Slocum's shoulder. His steel-gray eyes looked fuzzy as he tried to focus. "Go down there and take my horse. Tell them that Doc said, by Gawd, you could ride him up to that mine and back."

"I couldn't do that. Not take your good horse. Hell, the Apaches might steal it." Slocum wanted no party of borrowing the man's personal mount. There was no telling the value of the animal. And besides, Holliday was drunk as Hooter's goat. What would happen if he forgot he had offered it? Slocum didn't want some hemp noose closing in on his throat.

"Them red bastards might do it up there, but what the hell. By then they'd have roasted your nuts too, so you wouldn't give a damn." Holliday's laughter started him choking again. He spun around and coughed into his kerchief until his rasping breath left him wheezing.

"Take the son of bitch tomorrow. I don't need him," Holliday finally managed. "But if you come up and wake me about it, I'll shoot your ass off."

"I heard you," Slocum said, and ordered them another round. "Where's he stabled?"

"Pasco's." Doc tossed his head as if Slocum was supposed to know which way that was.

"Pasco's? I'm new in town."

"Block over, north of here. You can't miss it. Fremont Street."

"I'm in your gratitude," Slocum said.

"You will be Gawdamn lucky if that proud-cut bastard don't pile you on your ass. Tell me when you get back how shitting grateful you are, sah."

"I'll still be in your debt."

"Dodge City, huh?" Holliday shook his head. "Can't recall you, Slocum. Wyatt will. He ain't forgot the first time he wiped his ass. Hate that memory business. But I usually remember a real man." Holliday frowned at the sound of gunshots and shook his head.

"Damn cowboys shooting things up again."

"Cowboys?"

"Aw, hell, they ain't punchers. A bunch of two-bit cattle rustlers, stage robbers, that think they own this whole place. Old Man Clanton runs the deal. The son of bitch would screw his own dog. They think they can come up here and tree the town whenever they want." Holliday chuckled to himself over something private. "They're fixing to learn all about it. They're the kind that ain't got the guts to piss in the open. Stay clear of them, they'd rob you if there were ten of them. You know what I mean?"

"I appreciate the use of your horse." Slocum raised the glass, waiting to give the man a chance to back out on his offer.

"Hell, Slocum, I appreciate meeting you again. Even if I can't find you in my brain. See you when you get back. Maybe by then I'll remember you."

Slocum left the Oriental Saloon and headed for the stage office. In Dodge, he had not seen Holliday very much, so trying to remember would be useless. He would get his gear, sleep in the livery yard, and ride out at dawn. His boot heels clunked on the boardwalk as he avoided a couple of singing drunks arm-locked and cruising the porches. He glanced back toward Nellie Cashman's and wondered how Mrs. McClain was sleeping in her room.

"Howdy. Guess you come back for your gear?" the

freckled-faced youth said, standing in the stage line office's doorway.

"Yes. Any sign of Mrs. McClain's husband?" he asked.

"None. He never showed here. I've asked several guys about him," the boy said, and shook his head as if troubled by the matter.

"What did they say?" Slocum paused for the answer before he picked up his gear.

"They never heard of him."

"Maybe they weren't in those mountains where he's at?" He lifted the saddle by the fork and waited for the reply. There was plenty of country out there. You couldn't know everyone from east to west.

"No, mister. They know that range and they never heard of no McClain ever ranching in the Swisshelm Mountains."

"I sure don't know. Where's Pasco's livery?" Slocum asked. Mrs. McClain's plight seemed more serious by the moment. No ranch, no husband—what was going on? She sure was a lot of good-looking woman to be in such a fix. But it was none of his concern. He had a mine to see about.

"Pasco's Livery? You go up here to Fremont, turn right, and it's on the left past Sheflein's Hall." The boy pointed the way. "You can't miss it."

"Thanks," Slocum said as he considered the woman's plight. No ranch, no husband—she had mentioned how her husband was building up a herd. Thoughts of her shapely beauty made his stomach roil. He headed up the street as two drunks on horseback rode by singing a cattle-driving song about "Calinda."

"Oh, wait for me, sweet Calinda, I'll be home this fall. . . ." Their words trailed off in the night as they trotted their mounts away from him.

What had happened to her man? Slocum crossed the shadowy street where no light was shed on the hard-packed caliche. He passed the dark Chinese grocery on the corner, and finally saw the lamp hung outside the livery down the block. Maybe her husband wasn't coming back. Slocum adjusted the saddle on his shoulder. Not his problem.

3

"Mister, if you've lied to me about having permission to use Doc's horse, you better ride like hell, because you'll be in Hell that quick." The man snapped his fingers in Slocum's face.

"Do I look stupid?" He scowled at Lem Pasco. What kind of a fool did the man think he was anyway?

"Damned if I know. But it won't be my ass if anything happens to this horse."

"Doc said he might buck," Slocum said, nearly through saddling the animal. He jerked down the stirrup, and the leggy gelding shied aside. Still holding the reins, he let the horse drag him along a few steps before he adjusted him with a sharp jerk on the reins.

The horse was wide-eyed and blowing warily as Slocum coaxed him in a soft voice to hold still. His hand soon rubbed the velvet muzzle and felt the rapid breathing from the horse's flared nostrils, while his hard grasp on the bridle reins kept the horse from backing away. "Easy, big man, we've got miles to cover.'' The horse tossed his head, and then settled as if the wildfire had fled his whole body. It was time to mount up, and with the head stall close to Slocum's leg, he put his left boot toe in the stirrup and swung up in one fluid movement. His right toe found the other stirrup as the horse circled anxiously about in the empty street before the livery.

When he released the bridle, he had the reins gathered, and checked the powerful bay's actions into stiff-legged hops east on Fremont Street. Then the gelding tried to take the bits, but Slocum kept his chin pulled back low enough that he couldn't stretch his neck. Moving sideways down the street at a fast clip, the powerful horse could only strain his jaw at the strong hands holding him from bucking or, worse, busting loose in a wild race.

By the time they reached the Gleason Road, he was in a high-stepping trot and Slocum gave him more rein. He broke from a trot into a lope, and Slocum let him run off the hill to where the road turned up the dry wash. Then he checked him to a trot. Across the sandy crossing, Slocum short-loped him up the next rise, and on top the horse settled into a long trot. The sun, coming up orange, shone on the purple-red Dragoon Mountains piled ahead of him in the crisp distance.

Doc's horse was better than Slocum had even expected. An animal like this one was rare, and perhaps the slip of the knife had done Doc a big favor. Slocum knew the difference between cutting a stud and proud-cutting one amounted to fractions of inches, and only an expert could do it right. Most ranches hated proud-cut animals, because they caused trouble in the remuda, but for saddle horses they were sought after. Slocum didn't want to think about the value of the bay gelding. In a horse market like Tombstone's, he could easily bring five hundred dollars, and that would be a bargain.

At the base of the mountains, Slocum turned along the face and headed west until he found the military road that went over the pass. In the deepening gorge, he rode around some freight wagons pulled by oxen. The freighters waved and shouted to him as if glad to see another white man in passing. The smooth-tracking horse carried him quickly by them and up the road carved into the mountainside.

By ten on the sun time, he reached the side canyon of the Lucky Lady Mine. He let the horse walk up through the scrubby pines. Scolded by a few jays in the boughs, he took off his hat and scratched an itch in his scalp. The operation was a half mile or so away.

"Hold it right there, mister," someone challenged him a few minutes later. The man wore a four-peak hat with a flat brim, Apache boots, and canvas overalls. His shirt was coated in dust, and sweat circles darkened his armpits.

"That you, Ferd Forneau?" he asked, reining up the bay.

"Well, I'll be ticked. Hey, Monroe, get up here, the boss finally got back."

"About time," Monroe grumbled out of sight.

"We wondered when you'd get here," Ferd said.

"Well, I made it. How does it look?" Slocum asked, dismounting.

"Not bad. We think the latest rock is the best we've seen since we started." Ferd set the rifle aside and tossed Slocum a chunk of rock from atop the dump.

"By Gawd, he did come," the whiskered face said as Monroe showed himself above the top of the homemade ladder. Then the taller and thinner miner came out and dusted off his hands in a clap.

"Howdy, Monroe." Slocum extended his hand.

"Damn, been some hard digging here," Monroe said. Then they shook hands.

"This look good to you?" Slocum held up the sample.

"Hell, it's real silver ore," Monroe said with an edge of impatience.

"Worth packing out of this canyon?"

"Damn right it is. Maybe twenty or more ounces to the ton. Some of it may run higher than that."

"You think it's that high?" Slocum asked Ferd.

"Monroe, he knows that assay business good. I think maybe more, but he usually is right."

"Well, if we have a mine, what do we do next?"

"Get a bucket and mule, maybe a steam engine. Hire some high-grader to haul it to Charleston."

"You mean someone who will steal the best ore off the load and throw it off the wagon for his friends to find along the way and then they work the silver out for themselves?"

"By Gar, he learns fast," Ferd said with a broad smile.

"He ain't no pilgrim," Monroe said, and winked at Slocum.

"You bring any whiskey to celebrate this find?" Ferd asked.

"Got a few bottles if that bay ain't broke them jogging up here." Slocum rose to go get the bottles from the saddlebags. The bay jerked his head up from grazing through the bits and whinnied at him.

"So you want to make friends?" Slocum asked the horse with a grin as he walked by to the saddlebags for the whiskey.

The bay went back to snatching more dried grass. Then he raised up to chew and wad it into his mouth, clicking the bit as he ate. There was plenty for him to eat. The bay would be fine, busy grazing. Slocum headed back up the grade carrying the two bottles.

"Had any trouble?" he asked, climbing up on the ledge with the men.

"Been some, but we discouraged it."

"Claim jumpers?"

"They wasn't up here for no Sunday school picnic," Monroe said, taking out his jackknife to cut the seal on the bottle Slocum handed him.

"A winch, cable, a bucket, and that steam engine is going to require some capital," Slocum said. He was down to the part he had dreaded. If the mine proved, how in the blazes could he ever raise the capital to get it going? He wasn't exactly the prize sort of borrower bankers looked for to lend money. He had no address and no permanent residence to convince a money man how reliable he was. No, he'd have to do something else.

"Ain't a banker in the territory won't loan it to you on that high grade a ore." Monroe took a deep draught out of the bottle and then wiped his mouth on his dust-floured sleeve.

"Say, what if I make you two a deed for two thirds of this hole. What would you two do?"

Monroe blinked at his partner, who in turn frowned at Slocum's offer. He handed him the bottle with a wry set to his thin mouth.

"I don't understand, Slocum. This is your mine. We agreed to dig a shaft fifty feet deep for five hundred dollars. Ain't you got the money to pay us?" Ferd asked.

"Oh, I have the money, but due to some past events, I might not qualify for a loan."

"Why give us that much of the whole pie?"

"Yeah, who are *we*?" Monroe asked.

"My new partners in the Lady Luck Mine." Slocum hoisted the bottle that was handed to him in a toast to them, and then took a deep draught.

"By Gawd, you've damn sure got them!" Ferd shouted.

"You dang tooting. How does it work?"

"I give you a quit claim deed to the claim. You file it in Tombstone courthouse, get the assay report, and then go see the bankers. You boys know this business. I'm the dude."

"You know it may peter out in ten feet?" Monroe warned him.

"All you two owe me is one third of the profits, not the cost of running it."

"How in hell did you make this claim anyway?" Monroe held the bottle out, examining it, ready to take another snort.

"I stumbled on it when Tom Horn and I were meat-hunting up here a couple years ago. Before Tombstone burned the first time. We shot deer, javelinas, bear, antelope—hell, anything for meat to feed the town."

"By damn, she's a Lucky Lady all right. Partner," Ferd said to his co-worker. "We better get us a sack of this ore and round up that jasshonky of ours and get our butts to Tombstone."

"Yeah, yeah, we're half rich and you're already bossy as a wife."

"How in the hell will we find you for your part?" Ferd asked Slocum.

"If I'm not around," Slocum said, "then I'll drop you a line where to send it."

"Good," Ferd said, and nodded his head as if in deep thought about the matter.

"Something wrong?" Slocum asked.

"Oh, hell, no. We been thinking how to do this mining business for ourselves for so damn long. I just can't believe it's really happened." Monroe shook his head as Ferd rose stiffly and handed him the half-full bottle.

"By Gar, it's a saint's day for us." The Frenchman shook his head in disbelief.

"It damn sure is," Monroe agreed, scratching his neck inside his collar-less shirt. "I'll never forget it, nor your generosity."

"You may cuss me someday," Slocum said, taking the bottle and downing the remains.

"Be a cold day in Hell before we do that," Monroe said, and his buddy nodded his agreement. "Tell me one thing." He was looking hard at the grazing horse.

"What's that?"

"You ever give away your horses like you do your mines?" Monroe asked

"I can't. I borrowed it from Doc Holliday to get up here. I've got to take him back."

Impressed, Ferd whistled through his teeth. "In that case, I'd damn sure be certain he got back without a scratch. The man is pure hell when he's mad."

"Partners," Slocum said, scribbling his signature on the quit claim deed. He handed it to Ferd. "Here's my part. Now you two make it a mine."

They shook hands around, and then he gave them a

salute and headed for Doc's horse. If anyone could make the mine work, he had just made the sweetest deal in his lifetime. All his nights out with coyotes might just be paying off. Oh, he'd find Tom Horn sometime and settle with him too, but for the moment he was as rich as he'd been in his life.

He drew a deep breath, then went and caught the bay by the reins. In a vault he was in the saddle, and whirled the horse around to wave at the two men squatted on the rock-strewn dump, finishing the last of the whiskey.

"To all of us being rich as hell!" Monroe shouted after him, and he added an "Amen" as Slocum headed down the canyon.

When he reached the soldier road, he stood in the stirrups to let the bay trot. As he came off onto a long flat stretch, three masked men rode from behind some junipers with guns drawn.

"Reach for the sky!" came the order.

He quickly looked around for a place to escape, but knew he was under the threat of three revolvers—and even bad shots wouldn't miss at that close range. Slowly he raised his hands as the one on the sorrel rode in and took his pistol.

The bandits wore flour sacks over their heads and linen dusters to hide their clothing. One rode a bay with scars on his right front leg; another was aboard a well-muscled paint. He wouldn't forget their mounts.

"Damn nice horse you got there," the leader said. Then the lights went out, and Slocum didn't recall anything but the acrid taste in his mouth. He came around lying on the road with a helluva of a headache and lump on his head the size of an egg.

Raising up on his hand and knees, he spotted his hat on the ground; his holster was empty when he reached for it. His shirt was torn open, the money belt from around his middle was gone, and there was nary a sign of Doc's blood bay horse. He closed his eyes to the whole matter.

Then, with considerable effort, he rose to his feet. The

pounding in his head was so hard he wished for more whiskey as he sought his hat. Sweeping it up, he saw where the robber had dented it when Slocum was struck from behind with a gun barrel. He punched out the crown and set it on his tender scalp.

He was in a hell of a mess: broke, without Doc's good horse, and afoot twenty miles from Tombstone. Who were the robbers? He would need to think on that awhile. The leader rode a sorrel with a white sock, and there was a scar-legged bay and a white—no, a paint, he thought. Damn, his head hurt too bad to even think.

4

"Has Doc been in here tonight?" Slocum asked, bellying up to the Oriental bar. His mouth was too dry to draw any saliva. There was no sign of the pale-faced Southern son in the smoky room, but Doc might be out back in the facilities or down the street, taking part in the twenty-four-hour card game in the Bird Cage Theater's basement.

"Doc's gone to Mexico to see about some damned fighting cocks," the bartender said as he looked Slocum over with a concerned frown. Then he poured him a drink of whiskey. "You look terrible, man. What happened to you today?"

"It's been one a helluva a day. Here's my last buck, give me another shot," Slocum said with a wary shake of his head and then a quick check of the crowd in the barroom. "How the hell did he go down there?" He couldn't figure out Doc's mode of transportation, since Slocum had taken his saddle horse.

"Took a surrey and went with a guy called Greenley. What happened to you anyway?"

"Some masked bandits robbed me up in the Dragoons this afternoon and took Doc's good horse as well as my money." Slocum drained the second shot and slapped the jigger on the bar. "Who's the law in this place?"

"That would be Sheriff Johnny Behan's territory, I guess." The man wrinkled his nose. "He won't do very damn much. Probably one of his own men did it."

"He won't, huh?" Slocum frowned. His head still throbbed like a thunderstorm from the blow. "That figures. Where's Virgil Earp?"

"I can tell your right off that he ain't got any jurisdiction out of town."

"Don't matter if he knows who rode the horses I saw."

"Yes, I guess you're right." The barkeep raised his brows and conceded the point with a grim nod.

"Good, I'm headed for the marshal's office."

"What should I tell Doc about his horse?" the man asked in a low voice as he leaned close and refilled the glass. He nodded toward the small tumbler with a nod to let Slocum know that the shot was on the house.

"Don't tell him a thing. I'll tell him myself." Slocum hoisted the glass, gave the barkeep a grateful nod, downed it, and then wiped his mouth on his sleeve. The ride into town atop that ore wagon had been a bumpy, dusty ordeal.

"Thank God you're going to tell him. I'd hate like hell to have to. You be careful, mister. I believe you will tell him. Have another one on the house." He held the bottle out to refill the glass. "I figure I better let you know that Doc's due back here day after tomorrow."

"Good, it'll give me some time to find the rustlers," Slocum said, lifting the whiskey, and then he toasted the man. "Thanks. Here's to finding Doc's horse."

All his gear was gone, but they hadn't completely cleaned his plow. He had some money stashed in the lining of his boots that he would be forced to extract after he left the Oriental. It was no joke to be this bad off in an expensive place like Tombstone. He had to buy a new handgun too. He pushed through the bat-wing doors into the inky Tombstone night.

"Mr. Slocum, sir?" He looked at her in disbelief as she came forward from the edge of the porch into the slanting light from the saloon's interior that shone on the boardwalk. She wore a hood to conceal her face, and swept it back for him to see that it was the woman from the stage, Mrs. McClain.

"Yes, ma'am?"

"Could we speak someplace more private than this, sir?"

"Yes," he said, looking for a less busy place to talk with her. He ushered her down the boardwalk until they reached the front alcove of a respectable business closed and dark for the night.

"I heard at the hotel that you had returned to Tombstone," she said, avoiding his gaze.

"Yes, but I am all filthy and everything," he said, embarrassed at his state of dress.

"Never mind that, sir," she said to dismiss his concern about his appearance. "I have no one to turn to. My husband, Landon McClain, has obviously lied both to my family and to me."

"He's what?" He sheltered her with his body when two drunks went wagging arm in arm down the boardwalk, singing an explicit verse of a barroom song.

"And down from the mountain, from up on Bear Ass Creek, came a blue-balled bastard named Piss Pot Pete. Oh! He laid his rod upon Murphy's bar. I swear it stretched from here to thar. Gawdamn stink!" They broke into laughter at their clever rendition, and were soon out of hearing as they started on the second verse.

"Sorry," Slocum said, searching around for a better place for them to talk. "You shouldn't be here."

"I can assure you, sir. I have greater problems than a few drunks singing filthy barroom ditties."

"What kind of problems?" He glanced up and down the poorly lighted Fifth Street, but saw no one else coming to disturb them.

"Landon McClain was supposed to be building a ranch in the mountains that I mentioned to you."

"What *has* he been doing?" How had Slocum gotten into his mess with her anyway? He had enough problems of his own with Doc's expensive mount gone and all his own things stolen.

"I guess he's been spending my family's money on whiskey and women of loose morals." She shook her head in the dark shadows.

"I don't understand," Slocum said, frowning at the woman under the hood.

"My father gave him lots of money to start this ranch."

"And he has not done that?"

"No, and worse, I think he has joined a band of outlaws."

"You know all this for the truth?" He shook his throbbing head, then rubbed at the back of it. His actions tilted his hat and he was forced to reset it. What kind of scoundrel was Landon McClain?

"Yes, I do," she replied.

"Let's go to Nellie's. I need a meal. I'll have to get some money out of my boot lining somewhere between here." He didn't even have a jackknife—they'd taken that too. He wanted his hands on those three outlaws, his bare hands, so he could throttle them slowly for all this inconvenience they'd caused him.

"Do you need some money?" she asked.

"I'm afraid I do. Some robbers stole my money belt today and Doc Holliday's fancy horse. This has not been my best day."

"Mine either, I can assure you. Let me buy the meal," she offered.

"You are certain this husband of yours has taken the money and spent it?" Something sounded bizarre about this whole business. They started for Nellie's.

"I checked the records at the courthouse," she said. "He did buy a ranch."

"So you know that much? Let's cross the street. There

is a bunch gathering in front of the Oriental." He steered her across the street.

"Is something wrong?" she asked, frowning as she reset the hood against the gust of night wind.

"I have no idea. I simply want to avoid any sort of problem until I find those men who robbed me today." He tried to make out the loud voices of those gathered on the corner porch. Something was amiss, and he wondered what was wrong, but not enough to leave her alone to find out.

They crossed Allen, letting two cowboys ride past, then reached the far side. He glanced back at the crowd in front of the Oriental. Still wondering what that was all about, he turned back to her.

"Do you think the robbers that held you up today may be right here in Tombstone?" she hissed at him.

"Yes, I certainly think they are having a high old time in one of these saloons at this moment on the proceeds of the robbery."

"How many were there?"

"Three armed men." He looked back, and could make out nothing from the mob voices a half block away before he and Mrs. McClain went inside Nellie's warm, fragrant-smelling restaurant. The rich cooking aroma made him half sick at the thought of his hunger, but the bar whiskey had warmed him some. As the Chinese waiter seated them at a side table, Mrs. McClain said, "I have a map from the clerk's office on how to get there. Can I hire you to take me to the Swisshelm Mountains where this ranch is?" Her deep blue eyes looked like two smooth pools as she waited for his answer.

"I guess, but why?"

"I intend to see the land that he bought."

"I thought—"

"No, he bought land, but according to local people he's never worked the ranch. Instead he rode off with some ruffians."

"No cows then?" Slocum looked at her over the menu,

still confused about what his role would be in the matter. Meanwhile, her beauty stirred him inside.

"He never bought a cow, from all that I have heard. Unless he stole them."

"Did you speak to the sheriff?" Slocum asked as the waiter poured them coffee.

"Do you know Johnny Behan?" she asked in rising indignation. Her back was more rigid as she sat taller in the high-back chair. He could envision her bust line, which pressed against the material of the blue dress.

"No, ma'am. Him and the Earps are sort of on the outs is all that I hear."

"The man is no gentleman!" she said, and stuck her proud breasts out further as she drew her head up indignantly.

"He insulted you?" What was Behan thinking?

"He suggested that I go back down here to my hotel and he would come to my suite to take my deposition. Just how stupid did he think I was? I was in his office." She looked hard across the table at Slocum for his reply.

"No help then?" He threw his hands up and slumped in his chair. He scrambled to recover when he discovered that the waiter stood ready with his pad to take their order.

"Bring us steaks and the works. Good enough?" Slocum asked her.

"Good enough."

Doc's expensive horse was gone, and so were Slocum's money and personal possessions. Also, Mrs. McClain was deep in some kind of big trouble over an errant husband, but that was really none of his own affair. If those robbers showed up he would tan their hides. After this meal with her, he planned to check the hitch rail for those horses they'd ridden. Deep inside, however, he doubted his luck was good enough to find a trace of them in Tombstone.

5

The wind swept grit and dirt in to an uplift. A dingy cloud of dust obscured the Huachucha Mountains far to the south. The force threatened to tear Slocum's canvas jumper open as he humped over the dash of the buckboard and scowled at the Appaloosa's spotted rump between the shafts. He flicked him with the reins to get him back into a trot each time the gelding acted ready to drop down to a walk. From time to time, Slocum glanced over at the silent woman wrapped in the blanket against the cold.

He couldn't talk Mrs. McClain into staying in Tombstone while he went and checked out this ranch in the Swisshelm Mountains. The cold snap ushered in on the sharp wind would be short-lived, but his advice for her to stay in town had fallen on deaf ears. What was this freezing, bitter drive out there going to prove? He slapped the Ap on the butt at the first sign of his slacking again. The gelding tried to turn and see him, but the blinders on the bridle kept him from doing that.

"You hate that horse?" she finally said, amused, hugging her arms under the colorful woolen Navajo blanket.

"I don't trust him," he replied. The cranky horse was only looking for an excuse to act up, and Slocum wanted no part of his stupidity.

"Did Marshal Earp recognize the description of the robbers' horses?"

"He thought his brother Wyatt might know who owned the paint horse that one of them rode."

"Is he the law too?"

"He's either working for Wells Fargo as an enforcer or has a federal badge. The Earps have all kinds of connections with the feds." He reined the horse down to a walk to cross a dry wash.

"Federal badge?" She swept the whipping blanket away from her face.

"A U.S. deputy marshal's badge."

"You don't like him, do you."

"You mean Wyatt?" he asked, looking at her as the force of the wind tore at them. Then he turned back to cluck to the horse. "Wyatt and I had some cross words back in Dodge."

"You didn't answer me. You don't like Wyatt?"

"He don't like me." With that said, he set the horse into a trot uphill and squinted against the dust storm's stinging force. It was plain stupid for either for them to be making this trip. Doc's was horse gone, he would be mad as a hornet when he got back, and there was no way to replace the horse. What would going out there prove for her anyway?

"I've heard lots of things about my husband since I came to Tombstone, Slocum."

He nodded that he was listening to her, but suspecting that the dumb buggy horse was about to act up, he focused his attention on him. The Ap began to ring his short tail: Slocum slapped him hard with the lines.

"Get up there, stupid!" he said as he drew the lines back to do it again.

"Do you know the Clantons?" she asked.

"I've met Ike before. Their old man has a big spread south of Tombstone on the San Pedro River. I would consider them less than stalwart citizens and not above doing anything underhanded."

"My husband Landon rides with some of them."

"The Lowerys too?" He glanced at her in disbelief, still concerned the horse was fixing to act like a booger or throw a ring-tailed fit.

"I guess, but they told me—"

"Who's they?" He drew back and snapped the end of the rein on the horse's spotted rump as he scotched him to a halt in the middle of the road.

"What's wrong with him?" she asked with a frown.

"He's fixing to try and balk on us. I intend to change his mind. He's tried every other trick in the book on me and not one has worked so far." He rose to his feet on the buggy floor as the horse stood four square in the road. Slocum drew back the lines and, with the flip of his wrist, a single rein snaked forward and he snapped it so hard that white hairs flew from the horse's belly.

The Ap tried to explode, but Slocum savagely sawed him down with the bit, though the animal tried to surge away. Then Slocum drew back and popped him again, talking all the time in a soft, low voice.

"Easy, Ap, easy there, Ap."

This time he drew back before the horse could blow up. Then he cut the horse again in the tender flank area with the rein tip. The Ap tried to rear, but Slocum worked the reins and hauled him down. Then he whipped him a fourth time, all the while calling to the horse, who was really named Ap, never raising his voice. This time, the dancing gelding tried to buck to escape the pain, but he was contained by the harness, the shafts, and Slocum's strong hands on the reins.

"Get up," Slocum said softly, and then touched the horse on the back with the lines.

Fearful of another whipping and hearing the voice of the unseen driver, the Ap struck out down the road at a good level trot. With his stubby mane unfurled in the wind, he acted like a new horse, ready to do his part. The thin wheels rattled up the grade again, and Slocum knew that soon they could view the distant Swisshelms if the dust wasn't too thick.

"How did you learn that trick with the horse?" she asked, shifting herself on the seat beside him for a more comfortable position.

"A long time ago a man taught me that horses have a one-track mind. If you can ever sidetrack them from their own notions, then you can make them do your will. I'll have to admit that I wasn't sure at all that I could do that with him. He's been so soured by someone's poor handling."

"He's doing fine now." She smiled for the first time.

"For now anyhow. Tell me about this business of the Clantons and your husband," he said over the rattle of the iron rims on the gravel road.

She explained how she had learned that her man had joined the ones they called the "Cowboys." A vexed look at times crossed her handsome face as she told him about the stories she had heard concerning his criminal activities.

"Why did he turn to being an outlaw?" She looked at Slocum in pained disbelief. "They say he's wanted for a dozen stage robberies and horse stealing as well."

"Did you hear where he's at?"

"A place called Paradise. Have you ever been there?"

"Yes, it's the other side of the Chiricahuas," he said with a knowing nod. My heavens, the man had really gone wild out West. Slocum slowed the Ap as they crossed the divide and the road grew rougher, tossing them against each other as the rig swayed from side to side. Finally, on the crest, he pointed to the purple mountains in the dust-obscured distance.

"That's them."

"That's where we're going?" she asked, ducking in her blanket as the wind's attack increased.

"Yes, if old Ap here don't take a notion to balk again." With that he sent the horse downhill in a long trot. He wished there was a way that they could escape the wind, but they had a long ways to go. Perhaps in the mountains, they would get away from some of the force of it.

Two hours later, they entered a deep canyon and were out of the wind at last, and he drew up the Ap to let him breathe. He tied off the reins and then stepped down and helped her to the ground.

"Whew," she said, teetering on her legs. He steadied her, and their glance met as they stood close enough that he could scent her flowery perfume over the juniper's turpentine smell in the air. They stood frozen, looking at each other. Then she drew a deep breath and excused herself. He let her go.

Overhead a giant gnarled cottonwood rustled, and the small creek gurgled a trace of silver clear water over the smooth rocks in the narrow channel. The high spring sun shone warm on his jumper as he waited for her return. Grateful to be out of the forceful wind, he decided the snorting, deep-breathing Ap would stand there while he went for a drink.

On his knees beside the stream, he heard the beat of horses coming down the canyon. He rose without taking a sip and then looked for her. There was no sign of her. He watched concerned as three riders came down the narrow road that sliced the scattered live oaks, juniper, and yuccas. He checked the butt of the new Colt in his holster. Where was she? He hoped she stayed out of sight until these men rode on, or at least until he knew their business in these mountains and who they were.

"Hey, boys, we got us a pilgrim," Ike Clanton said when he reined up his sweaty horse. He rose in the stirrups, drove his hand deep inside the front of his trousers, and began to give his privates some healthy scratching. With a wrinkled suit coat, a filthy white shirt, and a week's beard stubble on his full red face, there was no mistaking him.

"I got the damn crabs from some Mexican whore," Ike announced, and the other two younger men laughed at his words as they sized up Slocum.

"He ain't no pilgrim, Ike," the pimple-faced younger one said with a scowl.

"Shit, Tyler. I can see that." Ike made an uncomfortable face, still gouging at his problem and standing up in the stirrups. "Mister, you ever had the Gawdamn crabs?"

"A few times," Slocum said, not letting them move apart.

"What the hell did you do for them?" Ike asked, withdrawing his hand.

"Only thing you can do for them."

"What's that?" Ike asked with a frown.

"Set them on fire."

"Oh, hell! I can scratch them sum-bitches easier than that."

"Suit yourself," Slocum said, never letting them even think that their presence bothered him one inch.

"We ever met?" Ike asked. Finished scratching, he leaned over the saddlehorn to peer at him.

"Once or twice."

"How come I don't know your name?" Ike's pig eyes narrowed as he consider him.

"Slocum's my name, Ike."

"Can't recall you." He shook his head, and then removed his weatherbeaten hat and combed his oily hair back with his fingers, still looking with a question at Slocum. "That's Pepper Bill and this here kid's Tyler Lee," he said as he replaced his Stetson.

"Nice to meet you," Slocum said with a nod, grateful that Mrs. McClain had remained out of sight.

"You got a claim up here?" Ike asked.

"Looking."

"Good enough. Damn shame. I thought we'd found a pilgrim to tree when I seen that damn Appaloosa in the shafts."

"That's all they had at the OK Corral to rent. I figured he would be easier to drive than ride."

"That would be for Gawdamn sure. Short-backed bastard would ride hard as anything. Only a damn stinking Apache would ever steal him, and he'd get so pissed off at how bad he rode that he'd eat the stiff-legged bastard before noon.'' Ike laughed at his own joke, and his men chuckled, probably because they felt they had to.

"Good luck on your business, Slo-cum," Ike said with a nod to the other two that he was ready to ride on. "And don't you ever screw no damn Mexican whores with the crabs either. Damn, they itch." He held up his horse to reach back down inside his pants to scratch his privates again. The other two were snickering as they left at a trot ahead of him.

Ike finally rode off, looking dissatisfied. He was forced to lope to catch the others. Then Slocum saw Mrs. McClain step from behind the junipers. She waited at his frown until they were out of sight, then crossed the road to join him.

"Did I hear you call him Ike?" she said, looking to the west in the direction they had disappeared.

"That was Ike Clanton."

"Just the sort of man a woman would want her husband to run with." She shook her head in disgust.

Slocum never answered her. He went to the stream and, crouched on his haunches, cupped up some water. Wary that Ike and his boys might circle back, he kept himself ready. She joined him, drawing up her skirt to sit on a flat rock beside the small stream.

"Water good?" she asked.

"Yes."

"Those men upset you, didn't they?"

He nodded woodenly. One thing he knew for certain: Ike Clanton was an opportunist and he used any chance he had to make selfish gains, legal and illegal. Slowly Slocum rose to his feet and studied the empty wagon tracks that led back toward Tombstone. He'd feel ten times better if he knew Ike's business in the Swisshelms.

They reached the wood frame shack close to noontime. Slocum drew up the Ap and studied the unfinished corral. Several peeled juniper posts had been set; others were merely stuck in holes and not tamped in. Set in a grove of live oak, the ranch headquarters was nestled deep in a side canyon. A Mexican mockingbird scolded them with his various obscene-sounding whistles and calls.

"Who is he?" she asked, grinning at the noisy bird.

"Mexicans got a name for him. Just a mockingbird, but he'll sure talk to you."

"It's a pretty place, isn't it?" she asked, looking around as he helped her down.

"A man might think so, but a woman from Chicago ought to want to get on the next stage for home." He considered her shapely backside as she headed for the shack.

"I have planned to live here for over a year," she announced as she paused to turn and look at him.

"Yes, but it is different now. Then you had a husband, or thought you did, to look after you out here."

"Landon started to do things here," she said, taking her skirt in hand and starting again for the small structure.

"I'd say he got tired and said to hell with it." Slocum decided that the man had become disappointed with arid ranching.

"You never really know a person, do you?" she asked.

"How is that?" He checked around to make sure there was nothing in sight, but the skin on the back of his neck itched. He rubbed it and then followed her.

"I met Landon at a social event. He was from St. Louis. Had been a cattle buyer there, then came to Chicago and met some of my friends. I was impressed. My father was impressed with Landon too. This wonderful land in Arizona, he told us. No winter, no need to make hay, grazing the year round. I must say I had to compete with my own father for this man."

"Had Landon ever been here?"

"Once, he said, but I don't know if it's true. He said he was here delivering live beef to the Army."

"People did that. They still do. You married him, right?"

"Yes. I wanted a big church wedding, but he said we should save that money and invest it in this ranch."

"He won out."

"Obviously." She carefully lifted the latch string, then shoved the door in with a loud creak and spray of dust and cobwebs.

"Whew, this hasn't been used in a while." she said as he caught her arm and pulled her back before she could step inside.

"What's the matter?" she asked wide-eyed.

"Could be a diamondback rattler inside there. They come in after mice and rats, you know."

"Oh," she said, her mouth forming a big O.

From the threshold, he checked inside the dark room. It smelled like musty socks. Finally he fished out a lucifer and struck it. He held the blazing match high for illumination, and seeing nothing on the hard-packed dirt floor between him and the table, he stepped inside.

"All clear?" she asked quietly.

"Just be careful." He motioned for her to stay back as he lit another match to torch the wick on a small stub of a candle atop the table.

"This place stinks like old shoes," she said, coming close on his heels and looking all around.

"It isn't roses," he teased, and looked carefully at the rest of the room.

"There's some canned goods." She pointed. "And a bed." Her voice trailed off as she looked across the room at the small cot piled with a few tattered handmade quilts.

"I'll go take care of the horse. Watch carefully what you do and what you turn over in here while I'm gone," he said to her.

"I will," she promised, and began with a deep interest to examine every item as if there might be some answer in it for her.

Convinced that she would be all right for the time being, he went outside and unhitched the Ap from the rig. He piled the harness in the back of the wagon, and then fitted some rope hobbles on horse's front legs. He turned the gelding loose to graze. There was water in the draw and plenty of feed for him; new green sprouts were coming out of the winter-cured bunches of grama grass. He was satisfied that the Ap wouldn't go anywhere. Suddenly a shrill, bloodcurdling scream from the house forced him to whirl around.

His boot heels barely hitting the ground, he rushed for the house and the panic-stricken woman inside.

6

She rushed out the doorway, terror in her eyes. He caught her in his arms and frowned down at her pale face. He felt the ripeness of her body in his embrace as he searched her fear-stricken face for an answer.

"A—long-tailed thing—" Her right arm flung back to indicate the interior of the shack.

"A scorpion?" he asked, hugging her tight to his chest.

"I—think so—it was in the bedclothes. It was—over a foot long."

"They aren't the bad kind," he said, savoring her closeness. The hint of perfume whirled up his nose. "The little ones are more poisonous than those big fellows. That's why everyone dumps their boots out before they put them on in this country."

He could feel the rapid beat of her heart against his chest. Her breath was coming in deep heaves. Her muscles involuntarily shuddered in his embrace as he bent over so his mouth met hers. He thought of the one word that summed up her state. Vulnerable. He tasted the honey sweetness of her lips, Then she tore her face away and hugged him harder.

"What am I doing?" she asked in his ear.

"Whatever you want." He waited for her to go on.

"Slocum?" she asked in a little girl's voice.

"Yes."

"Be gentle. I—I may cry."

"We can stop." He wanted her to have one more chance to deny him if that was her wish. As fired up as he was, he hoped she didn't—but it would be her choice.

"No. Right or wrong, I want to."

"Good." He began nibbling on her neck under the clean-smelling hair. Then, with a deep breath, he reached under her, lifted her up in his arms, and swept her over the threshold.

"Can we go outside?" she asked, pleading with her blue eyes.

"We better take a blanket."

"No, they're sour and stink." She wrinkled her nose at the notion.

"There might be thorns on the ground," he said, turning and facing the sun lit doorway.

"I don't care," she said, and hugged his neck. Her wet mouth kissed him on the face. He strode from the cabin carrying her lithe form across the yard. A shady patch of matted-down grass looked like the place to set her down. He knelt to ease her down. Her long fingers framed his face and she sought his mouth as he continued to hold her in his arms. The sun dimmed its glare as he closed his eyes, tasting her sweetness.

"The Navajo blanket would do," she said, and he released her, easing her feet to the ground. She ran to the wagon and came quickly back. A vision of her slender firm body under the blue material excited him.

She whipped the colorful cover in the air and then spread it on the ground. They both knelt and faced each other. An unquenched fire shone in her eyes.

In their hungry search, they quickly sprawled on the

hard weaved blanket with her atop his chest. His hand
tested her hard right breast through the material, and fire
swirled his brain. Finally out of breath, they parted, rising
up to their knees. He undid the cumbersome holster while
she stripped the vest off his shoulders. Next, she fumbled
with his shirt buttons until her fingers sought entry and
rushed over his chest. Exploring and massaging the
corded muscles of his belly, she closed her eyes as if to
savor what she discovered.

Weak with need for her, he undid the small buttons on
her dress front with unwilling fingers. Damn, he couldn't
recall in years being shaken with so much anticipation to
liberate the rock-hard mounds under the material. Her
dress was finally open to the waist, and he found a frilly
lacy layer keeping him out. He undid the camisole buttons, and soon exposed the long pointed pair, capped by
dark brown nipples that hardened like rocks at the gentle
touch of his fingertip.

He raised the right breast in his palm as if weighing it.
Then he bent over and slowly began to sip on it. She cried
out loud and hugged him to it. In a minute, she was
sprawled on her back. Her eyes shut behind thick brown
lashes, she was fast drowning in the same fire that consumed him. He knelt over her, testing the other breast with
his mouth. With his palm under her dress, he rubbed the
satiny inside of her legs as she eased them apart. He finally reached the wet vortex and she stifled a cry.

"Please take me," she whispered.

He rose up and toed off his boots, regretting the lost
time required as he looked down at her while she raised
her snowy legs for him. He shucked off his pants inside
out, then his underwear, and finally stood on one foot at
a time to strip away his socks.

A slow smile of pleasure crept over her face as he knelt
at her feet and gently spread her knees. Her long breasts
stood upright in the tree-filtered sunshine that shone on
them. He leaned forward and kissed her pursed lips as he
scooted his knees forward. His ample manhood nosed into

her gates and slowly, despite the urgent need in his hips, he began to enter her.

Her mouth formed an O. She cried out as he went deeper, and then she started arching her back under him for more. They were soon meshed as one, and like a wind-tossed field of green wheat they began to rise and fall in a symphony. Their efforts grew fierce. Her fingernails dug in his back as she clutched him for more. Abandoned to her need, she pressed her hips to meet his grinding need and unsubdued desire.

He sought her in the surges of her passion. Higher and higher they went. Then she found release and fell limp for a half second. Her moments of stillness were quickly refueled into new fury as his intensity and mounting drive continued on top of her.

"Oh, yes," she cried as his tool reached a greater circumference of turgidity within her muscular convulsing tunnel. He felt ready to burst from the oversized head to the swollen base of his manhood. Then they collided in a crash that turned the brilliant day into darkness for both of them. Like a cannon shot from a ship deck, deep inside the cavern of muscular action he sent forth a hot explosion that went on and on forever with a depleting force that drained the last vestige of strength from both of them.

"Don't go away," she mumbled, and pulled him to her.

"I won't," he said, listening to the horse snort and the topknot quail's *whit-whew* whistle off in the brush. It sounded like they were alone. He hoped they were as he closed his eyes, savoring her wet kisses and her firm form pressed to his bare skin. Damn, he was too weak to do a thing.

He reached past her and put his thumb over hers to cock the Colt's hammer. If she was so damn intent on staying, she needed to know how to use a gun. The action locked in place, and he whispered for her to take aim and then squeeze off the trigger. The revolver bucked in her hand, and dust flew to the left of the line of brown bottles he had set up for her to shoot at beyond the unfinished corral.

"Damn, I missed," she said, making a perturbed face over her shoulder at him.

"Do it again, Mrs. McClain," he said without thinking. "This time imagine it's your finger and point it."

"My name's Lucia. Please call me that?"

"Lucia. Pretty name. I almost wish I'd known it before."

"Why?" She held the heavy gun before her like a pendulum in both hands.

"Nothing special, just nice to know you, Lucia." Then he smiled to set her at ease. It was nice to know the first name of a woman you'd made such violent love with. Lucia, huh? Whew, his head was still dizzy from their torrid time on the Navajo blanket.

Satisfied with his meager answer, she strained to rearm the handgun. Finally she used both of her thumbs to cock it, then steadied her aim and fired it. A bottle shattered in a million shards, and a small grin turned up the corner of her mouth.

"Just luck," he said, and motioned for her to continue.

Determined, she rearmed the Colt. Her next shot sprayed the bottles with grit, and she frowned disappointedly as she recocked the six-gun.

"Do you think I will ever learn how to shoot?"

"You're doing good for the first time. A smaller caliber would be better, but if you learn on a big bore like that .44 there, you can always handle a smaller one."

She hit the top of a bottle with her next round, sending the neck flying. Then her last shot went wild and slapped the ground above the row of targets.

He took the Colt and showed her how to eject the empty shells, and then reloaded five rounds in it, saving the empty chamber to rest the hammer on.

"What else will I need to learn stay up here?"

"Damn, I can't think of everything. This place is too crude for a woman that's used to civilization." He wished he had never even shown her how to shoot. It had only reinforced her desire to live up there. It was stupid for a city girl like her, raised in society, to even consider such a notion.

"I can live here as well as anyone."

"Oh, I can just see you milking a cow." He shook his head in disbelief as he considered her doing such a task. "Do you have any money?"

"Do you need more money?" she asked, looking concerned.

"No, but if you can afford it, I'll go to Mexico and get a family to come up here and help you."

"What would they cost?" she asked in her little girl's voice.

"Perhaps twenty a month and food."

"Oh, I could afford that. What could they do?"

"All the durn things you think you can do." He hugged her shoulder to cheer her.

"When do we go get them?"

"First, you must go back to Tombstone. I'll ride to Mexico and find the help there. When we get this shack ready, you can come up here."

"No!" She grabbed his arms and forced him to face her. "I want to help do some of it."

"You can't go to Sonora, period. I need to go down there by myself."

"I'll stay here then."

"No, not with Ike Clanton and his bunch roaming these mountains."

"That man is dangerous."

"Yes, he is. Ike's smart as a fox. He has no manners and reminds me of a boar hog, but he's not stupid or crazy either one. He's a cowardly mean man. Never underestimate Ike, never do that." Ike Clanton could be as cagey as any man he knew when it fit his purpose, and he would rape any woman as attractive as her in the drop of a hat, especially if he thought he could get by with it.

"I'll go back to Tombstone." She slipped her arm in the crook of his as they walked back to the shack. "But only until those people come here to work for me. I didn't mean to upset you."

"You didn't upset me. I'm simply concerned that you won't give up this entire notion of ranching up here."

"I won't give up that idea."

"What will you do if your husband comes back here?" he asked.

"I'll cross that river when I come to it."

"He's liable to, you know that?"

"Yes," she said softly.

He glanced over at her, but she was looking at the toes of her slippers. It was time he harnessed up the Ap and they headed back. It would be dark by the time they reached Tombstone. He wanted to stay there forever with her, but in reality he had lots of work to do. Maybe down in Sonora he could hire a good family for her.

She spun on her heels when they reached the porch and faced him. Then she turned her face up to kiss him. Her arm encircled his neck and her mouth tasted sweet and hungry; he found his own breath fast depleted. Finally, straining for air, they parted.

"We have to get back," he said, and closed his eyes to the thought of what he was denying himself. Damn, she was some woman. He let his breath out slowly as she went inside. To calm himself, he dug out a short cigar from his vest pocket, lighted it, and drew deep, letting the smoke fill his lungs. They had to go back. He closed his eyes to reality, letting the smoke escape his lips in a small stream.

7

Slocum got down from the Ap and tied him to a juniper bough. He had to be close to the camp of those who robbed him. The snitch in town that Virgil Earp had sent him to see had described this as the way to their camp up in the Whetstone Mountains. For five bucks, the nervous man had told him that the one who rode the paint horse and the two others were holed up above Grinder's Spring.

The tracks and the horse apples on the canyon's floor were fresh enough, and the pungent smell of wood smoke keep twitching Slocum's nose on the downdraft. They weren't being very secretive about their business, but who would bother them anyway? Not the Cochise County sheriff, that was certain. Not from all Slocum had heard about Johnny Behan. As Virgil Earp had told him, Belan made over thirty thousand a year just for collecting taxes and fines for the county. And that didn't count the rest of his lucrative deals with the outlaw element.

Making his way on foot up the draw and keeping to

the cover of the brushy junipers, Slocum wondered how many of the robbers were in camp. He paused often to listen and to try to spot them. He had no intention of walking right in on them before he sized them up. There might be more guns in there than he wanted to tangle with. More than anything else, he hoped that Doc's horse was there.

He looked forward to riding the bay again and leading the Ap. Through perseverance and sheer determination, he had made the stubborn Ap come this far from the OK Corral. Damn stupid horse anyway.

Slocum stopped. He could hear voices of men talking loudly to each other. Colt in his hand, he slipped behind a bushy evergreen to try to locate the talkers.

"—damn dumb sum-bitch," someone said. "Everyone knows who he belongs to. No one wants to buy that proud-cut bastard."

"How the hell did I know it was Doc Holliday's horse. I'd never seen the horse or that drifter riding him before."

"Take a good look as you raise your hands," Slocum said, and stepped out with his Colt drawn.

"It's him!" The younger outlaw blinked in disbelief.

"Turn around," Slocum ordered with a wave of his gun muzzle. He slipped in close and disarmed both men. Wedging their side arms in his waistband, he stepped back. "Who else is up here?"

"You'll find out soon enough," the older one snarled.

Slocum drove his gun's barrel hard into the outlaw's back. "You'll be the first to die when they try something. Better call them in and do it quick."

"Just a kid," the man said disgustedly.

"Call him in here."

"Tommy Jack, get your ass down here!"

"What you going to do with us?" the younger outlaw asked.

"Lynch you," Slocum said as a shocked boy in his teens came in view with an armload of wood. His freckled face turned ashen white at the sight of Slocum. He dropped the sticks and then looked bug-eyed at the sight of Slocum's gun, mechanically raising his hands high over his head.

"Mister, you talk damn tough," the oldest one said.

"What's your name?" Slocum asked him, waving the boy over to stand with the others.

"Leroy, Leroy Foley."

"Yours?" he asked the other outlaw.

"Tater Poage."

"What happened to Landon McClain?" he asked, hoping for some knowledge of the man's whereabouts.

"If he ain't died of lead poisoning, he's mending up at Sarah's. You a damn bounty dog?" Foley asked.

"At Paradise?" he asked, refusing them any information. This was his game and he held the aces.

"Yeah, that's where she keeps her shiny ass."

"Word's out that he's in bad shape?"

"Took a twelve-gauge charge in the guts from the stage guard north of Silver City. Why you so damn interested in him?"

"I know some of his relatives," Slocum said, motioning for them to kneel on the ground.

"McClain claims he's got lots of rich relatives."

"What the hell is he robbing stages for then?" Slocum asked.

"For the fun of it, I guess." Foley shrugged as Slocum knelt behind him and bound his hands.

"How much money you got on you?" Slocum asked, resting on his knee, waiting for a reply before he moved on to thrust up the other two.

"Maybe thirty dollars."

"Tater, how much you got?" he demanded.

"Maybe ten dollars. Why?"

"You boys owe me about over five hundred dollars as well as my guns and rifle. How do I get it back?" He figured they'd had enough time to squander the money he had raised to pay Ferd and Monroe for the shaft if they didn't take his partnership deal.

"Damned if I know," Tater said smugly, not looking at him.

Slocum rose swiftly, rushed over, and kicked the kneeling outlaw hard enough to send him sprawling on his face. It was one thing to rob a man, another to act smug about it.

He searched each one of the outlaws thoroughly, but soon realized as Poage fearfully turned his pockets inside out, they'd lost or spent a large amount of it.

"You better start thinking how I'm getting my money back. My patience is on a short fuse."

"Hell, I ain't got anything else," Tater groaned, holding his side.

"What did you do with the money you took off me and what you got out of my gear?"

"We gave Ike—"

"You better shut up, stupid!" Foley warned.

"You gave Ike half of it?" Slocum dragged Tater up to his knees, choking him by the collar of his shirt in the process.

"Yeah, we gave—him half."

"Foley," Slocum shouted at the man before he could stop Tater from telling him more, "you say another word, you'll have my boot toe in your teeth." Slocum shook Tater by the shirt front. "How many of you are there?"

"I—don't know what you mean?"

"That work for Clanton?"

"I ain't sure. Honest, I ain't sure."

"I'm taking your rigs, your horses. You three better hotfoot it out of this country. The next time I'll shoot first and ask questions later." He threw the man down on the ground before he did something he might regret. After cooling off some, he tied up Tater's hands behind his back. Finished, he shoved him face-down in the dirt to make his point, that he didn't intend to mess with them again.

Next, he bound up the trembling teen. Near the point of breaking, the youth could only chatter his yellow teeth despite the heat in the canyon. His words were incoherent.

"Son, if you know what's good for you, you better find a new vocation," Slocum said privately to the boy.

"I—will—"

Slocum shoved the money he had gathered in his front pants pockets, even pulling their boots off and finding ten dollars more hidden in their smelly socks. Then he saddled the four horses, lengthening the stirrups on the saddle that he chose to replace his own. He drew the sullen looks of the older robbers when he finally mounted up on Doc's spirited horse.

"Remember what I've said. Don't let me see your faces in Cochise County again. I won't hesitate to kill any one of the three of you next time we meet." He swung the prancing gelding around, leading the other three. He planned to pick up Ap on the way out. The other three were good horses. By his calculations the outlaws still owed him a lot of money plus the value of his gear. He figured it was the best he could do. As he rode out he said over his shoulder, "You all better be gone from here if you like to live."

It was late past sundown when he rode up Fremont Street and turned into Pasco's stable. The man came out of the office and blinked his eyes in disbelief.

"I'll be sum-bitch, you did get that damn horse back. I never figured that you could. Whose horses are those?"

"Mine. Repayment for the robbery."

Pasco whistled through his teeth. "You took them off some of those Cowboys, right?"

"Sure. They stole my gear and horse, then they spent my money. I guess turnaround is fair." He dismounted heavily, holding the saddlehorn until he got used to standing again.

"It might be fair, but . . ." Pasco lowered his voice to a whisper. "I'm warning you now that Ike Clanton will be gunning for you if you messed with his boys."

"Put my horses up and send anyone that asks about them to come see me."

"You're the boss. They didn't hurt Doc's horse none from the looks of him."

"They couldn't sell him. He was too damn famous."

Slocum laughed as he jerked the Winchester out of the boot. Not a bad long gun. He could use it.

"You have an appointment?" Pasco asked with a grin, holding the horses by the reins.

"Yes, and I'll take that paint and ride him tomorrow. Grain him good. And see if you can sell some dumb gold seeker that Ap."

"I think all of us with liveries have owned him. How much for him?"

"Get me seventy-five for him."

"Would you turn down fifty if I find a real sucker?"

Slocum considered the notion. Finally he nodded and started off in the dark across Fremont Street for Nellie Cashman's restaurant. He never stopped to consider the Oriental and all the noise coming from the barroom.

He almost collided with Virgil Earp at the corner.

"Excuse me, Marshal," he said.

"Going big-game hunting?" Earp asked, motioning to the long gun in his hand.

"No, but I've been hunting and found those galoots robbed me up in the Dragoons."

"You've chosen sides, huh?" Earp's dark eyes surveyed everything in the street as the two men stood in the shadows beside the path of light coming from under the bat-wing doors.

"I sent those three packing on foot. If that means choosing sides, then I did it today."

"Good, three less to worry me. I spoke to Wyatt."

Slocum listened. He had asked no favors of Virgil, though he appreciated the information about the snitch. What had Virgil spoken to his brother about?

"I spoke to Wyatt, and he said to tell you that Dodge was behind all of us. We've got enough problems here with the lawless element to not fight with any others."

"Tell him what's done is done and over for me too."

"Good. Doc gave him hell about his attitude toward you too. Holliday likes you. He laughed when they told him that the Cowboys robbed you and took his horse. Said they'd rue that day and he was right."

"Tell him that his horse is back in his stall and sound."

"I'm sure he'd like to hear it from you." Earp tossed his head toward the Oriental's noisy barroom.

"No, you can. I have a lady waiting down the street. Hate to keep a good-looking one waiting."

"Don't do it. I'll tell him. He wasn't concerned."

"Good, and thanks for the lead."

"Who was it?"

"Foley, Poage, and a pimple-faced kid."

"I know them. Good, that makes three less that Ike can count on."

"Night," Slocum said, and crossed Allen Street. As he ambled down the sidewalk, an arm reached out and dragged him into a dark storefront doorway.

"I was worried to death about you," she whispered, snuggling close enough that he could smell her perfume.

"I'm fine," he said, hugging her with the rifle in his hand.

"But it must be ten o'clock—" His mouth silenced her as he sampled the honey sweetness of her lips. He closed his sun-fried eyes and savored the willowy ripe body pressed to him.

Finally out of breath, he straightened and drew a drew deeply of the desert-smelling air on the night wind. They'd better eat before Nellie shut the place down.

"We better get inside before they close," he said.

"You need to hire those people and get the ranch fixed up so we have a place to be alone," she said under her breath as they hurried to the cafe's front door.

"Tomorrow I ride to Sonora to see about them. It will be a week before I can get it ready."

She hugged his arm, and he received the message. He wondered how he would tell her. He needed to share the information he'd learned earlier about her husband's condition. There was no reason to keep it from her.

"Your husband is badly wounded," he said quietly, leaning across the white linen tablecloth when the Chinese waiter went for their coffee.

She frowned. "How bad?"

"Those men that I recovered Doc's horse from today said he was shot during a stage robbery near Silver City."

"How could he do that to me?" Her blue eyes filled with concern as she warily shook her head.

"They say he bragged about his rich relatives. He's at Paradise, or was."

"I don't have a husband any longer." She clasped her hands together in the center of the table as if she had just made a big decision. "If he lives or dies, he's not my husband any longer. I'm getting a divorce. You can get them in the territory. I spoke to a lawyer today."

"Yes, ma'am."

"Slocum, don't you patronize me." She closed her left eye and glared threateningly at him.

"I won't."

"Good," she said with a wicked wink, and then let the waiter put the coffee cup before her.

With Doc's horse back and his own wealth more or less restored, he was ready to ride to Mexico and look for some ranch hands for her. His stomach was empty from a day without eating, and the food smells in the room drew the saliva to his mouth and made his belly churn. The only thing that might be better than a big meal would be to share a bed with her afterwards.

"Don't look now, but that Ike Clanton just walked in the door," she said softly with a scowl of disgust.

8

"Well—if it ain't my old friend Slo-cum." Ike's breath reeked of liquor and his yellowed teeth were exposed with his half smile. Then he blinked his pig eyes and quickly snatched off his hat at his discovery of Lucia. Unsteady on his boot heels, he teetered beside their table.

"Is this the Missus, huh, Slo-cum?" he asked, bent over almost in her face.

"Lucia, meet Ike Clanton."

Ike straightened and stuck out his chest. "I'm pleased to meet yeah, Luc—cia."

"Nice to meet you, Mr. Clanton," she said cold enough to chill the air in the room.

"I've had a little to drink this evening, so you excuse me, ma'am. But I must say you are sure fine looking."

"I'm certain you have a place to sit," Slocum said loud enough to gain Ike's attention, growing tired of the man's insistence on standing, weaving on his run-over boot heels and staring at Lucia with his whiskey breath in her face.

"Place to sit? Oh, yes, over there." He swung an arm off behind him with the too-long sleeve of the wrinkled, filthy suit coat he wore.

"You better find it, Ike."

He blinked at Slocum in disbelief. His thin mustache looked sparse, with curls of untrimmed hairs on his thin upper lip. Drool ran from the corner of his mouth, then down and off his stubbled chin. His red eyes glared in anger, challenging and full of malice like a prodded boar.

Slocum raised the barrel of the Winchester from the floor and poked Ike in the chest. As if instructed, he rose on his toes in silence under the gun's direction until he stood straight up.

"If you don't want your head blown off, go find your table and I'll forget this ever happened."

"Jesus, Slocum, do you know who I am?" He stood erect; he stared downward at the long gun's bore that almost touched his chin.

"Ike, I know what is respectable in front of a real lady. You're drunk. Leave."

"Did I offend—"

"Ike, get gone." He punctuated the matter with a shove of the gun muzzle.

"This ain't the end of this, Slocum." Ike's pig eyes half closed in furious anger; his fists opened and closed at his sides.

"It better be."

"It ain't," Ike growled and turned to join the other two at a table across the near empty diner. He stalked off.

"Slocum?" Lucia gushed, wide-eyed at the turn of events.

"I warned you. Tonight, you saw the animal in him." He put the Winchester back under the table, checking to see the still-angry man bitching to the others over his treatment. He didn't need any trouble with Ike in the cafe, but he wasn't going to let the man slobber and leer at Lucia like she was some common street slut either. He'd teach the man a lesson if he tried that again.

The boy brought their steaks and they both waited until

he was gone before they spoke again. Her face shone pale under the candlelight. He could see she had been shaken by the encounter. No one from Chicago society had ever seen such animal-like behavior from a human in a public place before either.

"You see why I wanted you to stay here in Tombstone."

She nodded woodenly.

"If Nellie was here she would have used a broom and run them off. She must be gone." He shook his head, letting the anger inside subside.

"She's in Tucson."

"Figures. You better eat," he said noticing her steak was still uncut.

"I doubt I can eat."

"Do you see what I meant now by the danger?"

"Yes. I purchased a smaller caliber pistol today."

"Good, get lots of shells for it. When we get up there, we will practice a lot more."

Lucia chewed on her lower lip and acted ready to say something. Then he saw the fear rise in her eyes. He was about to be attacked from behind. Instinctively, he ducked and then he sprung from his seat with an upper cut. His blow caught Ike on the chin and sent him staggering backward. Then, starting to rock back forward, Ike fell to his knees between two tables of startled patrons. Slocum grabbed a chair by the ladderback and swung it down on Ike's head as he struggled to rise up. The blow sent the man facedown on the floor.

"No fighty! No fighty!" the head Chinese waiter shouted, jumping up and down at a safe distance from both men.

Ike did not stir. Slocum glared at the other two. They shrugged in innocence.

"If you know what's good for him, take him home," Slocum ordered.

"We will," the one called Pepper Bill said. The two men dragged the limp Ike out as the upset Oriental employees cleared a way and even opened the door for their exit.

"Hey, you two," Slocum called after them, standing straddle his chair. "You pay them for the food and that chair I busted."

Pepper Bill looked about halfway angry, but dug the money from his pocket under his chaps. His unhappy glare was at Slocum the whole while he counted out the amount into the outstretched hand of the white-suited head waiter. Then he turned and left.

Slocum sat back down, satisfied that the problem was over. He drew in a deep breath to settle himself. His hunger gone, he doubted another bite of food would go past his tongue. He needed a drink and a cigar. Maybe later.

"It's all my fault," she said under her breath.

He shook his head to dismiss her concern. "It would have happened anyway. Ike and I were doomed to reach a settlement."

"Will this be the end of it?"

"No." Not with Ike Clanton. Nothing short of killing him would end that man's lust and pigheadedness. The blow from the chair would only put him out for the night. With Ike, there would always be a tomorrow. Besides, Ike still didn't know about him treeing and defanging his three men in the Whetstones that afternoon. No, he had more to come back about. Maybe a plot under the rocks over in Boot Hill Cemetery would be the only way to stop him.

After listening to all her concern and instructions for him to be careful, he left Lucia at the hotel and headed up the street for the Oriental. To keep from having more trouble, he left the rifle and his gun belt at the hotel desk. He recalled Virgil's unspoken concern about him packing irons within the city limits. The gun regulation was cut and dried and there was no need to strain his friendship with the law to let him off.

He pushed into the barroom and the fog of cigar smoke smarted his eyes. To his left, Doc looked up from the card game and grinned at him.

"Get over here, Slocum. I'm buying the whiskey."
Doc waved for him to join them. "They send word to-
night that hard-dick horse of mine is back at the stables.
Way to go."

"He's sound. I rode him back." Slocum accepted a
chair that Doc slung around for him. "Go ahead and play
your cards."

"Naw. They ain't worth a shit. They know I'm in a
losing phase." He gave a head toss to the others around
the table as he discarded the hand. "Who were the rustlers?"

"One was a Foley, a Poage and a kid."

"You kill them?"

"No, I tied a can to their tails and told them if they
came back I would."

"You should of sent them to hell." Doc shook his head
in disapproval. "That way they damn sure won't come
back and rob you a second time."

Then Slocum followed his gaze to the front door. The
marshal came inside the bat-wing doors and Doc waved
him over. "Hey, Virg, come over. The horse recovery
man is here."

"Howdy," the lawman said, taking another chair from
the empty table beside them and dropping down hard on
it. He raised his flat brim black hat and then wiped his
sweaty face on his black coat sleeve.

"Did you whip up on Ike tonight?" he asked.

"He was drunk and being obnoxious. Yes, I busted a
ten dollar chair over his head."

"Good for you. That little beady-eyed bastard needs to
be killed," Doc injected.

"They hustled him out to the ranch or I'd have arrested
him for causing trouble." Virgil looked disturbed by the
matter.

"Sounds like Slocum here did you a bigger favor."

"Yes, but we don't need any trouble in town the next
few weeks."

"Why's that?" Doc demanded.

"They said some big bankers were coming. Money

folks from back East and this town always needs lots of capitol. If they think this is some kind of helldorado they might not invest here."

"I won't fight with him anymore in town," Slocum promised Virgil as Doc handed him a glass of whiskey. He sent the bar girl after some cigars for all of them.

"Two guys came in from the Dragoons today," Virgil said. "They had some high grade ore."

Slocum wondered if they were his partners that brought the samples. But rather than bring any suspicion on his connection with them, he didn't bother to ask. He certainly could use some more money, but he had no intention to ask Lucia for any.

"That damn Wyatt head up there?" Doc asked with a scowl.

"I think so," Virgil said, shaking his head at Doc's offer of whiskey. "Slocum, you better watch your back. The damn Clanton bunch will be gunning for you from here on. They're back shooters, too."

The bar girl, who was hardly in her teens, returned with the jar of cigars. Slocum drew out several and paid her, offering one each to Doc and Virg who both waved off his offer, so Slocum stored the others in his vest pocket. A match struck under the table ignited the one he had bit the end from and soon the soothing nicotine settled his lungs and the good whiskey warmed him.

The bar girl returned and quietly offered to sit on his lap. He shook his head and she started to leave.

"Hey, girl, you ain't seen his pretty lady have you?" Doc asked after her.

"No," she said softly, turning to look at them.

"By God, his lady, she's from fine cloth, I mean to tell you," Doc said, then became caught up in his coughing.

"They get younger and younger working in these places," Virgil said.

"Maybe we're getting older?" Slocum asked with an elbow to the man. He watched her over the rim of his glass as she tried to imitate the older ones' swinging walk across the room. She had a long way to go; somewhere between innocence and experience and not real good at either one of them. Shame Bat Masterson wasn't there; he liked twelve-year-old ones. This girl wasn't much more than that.

"Maybe we *are* getting older," Virgil said as he rose and excused himself, then left the saloon to make his patrol.

"That damn Ike needs killing," Doc said as if considering the notion for the first time. "Where are you off to next?"

"Mexico."

"Why hell, I just come back from there. You be back here Sunday. I've got me the meanest set of roosters in this country. I aim to show these bastards around here Sunday what cock fighting is all about."

"I'll try to be back." Slocum rose and stretched his arms over his head.

"You leaving already?" Doc frowned in disapproval.

"Yes, I need some sleep."

"Better watch for that damn Ike; he'll be hot to even the score with you," Doc said with a wry head shake. "Sum-bitch needs to be killed."

Slocum could hear Doc's deep coughing clear out on the boardwalk over the sound of tinny pianos and some whore's loud singing down the street. Damn, Holliday was in bad shape. How long could he last? And Wyatt had gone to the Dragoons to see about the latest strike. *Sorry, big man, but that one's mine.* He headed for the Pasco's. He'd find a place in the haystack to sleep. In his financial shape, he didn't need to blow two dollars on a bed-bug infested hotel room. Besides, a million stars were out, and it would be warm till near dawn anyway.

9

Felippe, Sonora, Mexico

He rode the paint horse up the narrow road, passing several young women going to the village with jars of water balanced on their heads. A quick check showed nothing threatening in the dusty street; he dismounted in front of the windowless adobe marked *Cantina* in black faded letters. He hitched the horse, and was quickly surrounded by several beggar children dressed in rags.

"Señor, you want a *puta*?" the ambassador for them asked.

"No, why don't you go play," he said with frown at the youth's business. Then, noting the poverty of the children, he reconsidered his dismissal. "You want candy?" he asked all of them.

"Yes, yes!" the others shouted as he waved a young man in an apron over from the doorway of the store across the street. He gave him fifty cents and instructed him to give all of the children some candy. They surrounded the clerk shouting their orders. Someone even shouted their thanks to Slocum from the store doorway.

He hitched the reins on the rack. When he straightened, the same dark-eyed boy was there with his plea.

"Señor, it is my business to find work for her."

"Not today," he said, and headed inside the saloon. The boy was certainly persistent.

"What will it be, amigo?" the large man behind the bar asked.

"Whiskey or something good."

'The whiskey, I must warn you. She is horse piss." The man waited for his next choice.

"Give me the cactus juice then."

"Ah, señor, you will like this new stuff."

"Good." Slocum glanced back at the barefoot boy from the street, who had slipped into the bar and stood with his back to the wall by the door.

"There is no one in here needs to be screwed. Go on," the bartender said to the youth, shooing him outside before he poured the drink for Slocum.

"His mother?" Slocum asked as he finished lighting one of his cigars.

"No, his sister. They are orphans. The gringo bandits murdered their mother and father for little or nothing."

"What's his name?"

"Rafael, and his sister is Maria."

"How old is she?"

"About the boy's age." The man wrinkled his nose. "It is shame, but what can they do for work, huh?"

He'd heard enough. Slocum carried his drink to the doorway and parted the doors. There ought to be room on the ranch for two orphans, never mind the fact that they didn't need to live like this.

"Rafael," he shouted, and the boy jumped to his feet racing to the door.

"*Sí, señor.*"

"Go get your things and your sister. Do you have some burros that you and your sister can ride?"

"I can steal some."

"No." He frowned at the youth's answer, and began to dig money from his pants. "Here, go buy some. Then you two be ready to ride." He handed him a few dollars for the purchase.

"Where will we go?" Then boy's eyes narrowed in distrust of even such a magnificent benefactor.

"*Del norte.*"

"Oh, *sí*. You have hacienda we can work on?" The boy's face lighted up with excitement.

"Sort of. It is a ranch."

"It will be fine. My sister, she is very pretty, you won't regret it."

"I'm not—" He stopped. There was no need to tell him that. They'd learn the truth fast enough. "This is a real job that pays money and food."

"Oh, *sí*. We will be right here when you are ready to leave, *patron*."

Slocum turned and went back in to the bar. He let the man refill the glass with the sharp cactus juice. Lucia could use some help around the house. Those two would do fine. The boy would anyway. Hell only knew what the poor girl was like, but maybe Slocum had guessed right. He had enough intuition to think he had.

"I need a good *vaquero* to go north," he said to the bartender. "One who can make adobes and will build corrals too."

"This man I know has a big family." The man nodded his head that he was satisfied this would be a good choice.

"You mean many mouths to feed."

"*Sí,* many children, but they will work too."

"Where is this man?"

"I can send word to him."

"Send him word that I want to speak to him," Slocum said, and took the bottle from the bartender. He slapped down a silver dollar for it. It might run into hours to find this man. He decided to find a table to sit at.

"What's his name?" Slocum asked.

"Jose Morales," the barkeep said, taking off his apron.

Obviously he was going after the man himself. "He only lives a block away. You need more tequila, you help yourself, señor."

"*Gracias,*" Slocum said, and sat down on the chair.

Underneath the doors popped Rafael, and quickly he searched warily for the bartender. Slocum waved him over.

"He's gone," Slocum said. "Did you bring your sister?"

"Oh, *sí.* She said she would wait outside. She does not like this place."

"I'll go out there and meet her."

"No, since he is gone I will have her come in here to see you." In a jump he was out the doors, and returned dragging a reluctant girl who was wrapped in a colorful blanket.

"I will show you her beauty," he announced excitedly.

"No," Slocum said, waving her closer with his fingers, realizing she wore little or no clothing under the blanket. "Maria, you go to the store buy yourself a skirt, a blouse, and some sandals. The señora will want you properly dressed."

"Your señora?" she asked, her brown eyes wide in shock at this news.

"Yes." There was no need to tell her that the señora wasn't his. He held out the money to the slip of the girl. Her small brown hand unfolded and she accepted it.

"You were pleased with her, no?" Rafael demanded, looking puzzled at the money in her hand and their conversation.

"I am pleased if both of you work hard for the señora."

"Oh yes, we will work hard, *patron.* Be right back pronto with new clothes," he said. Then, with him talking to her at about a hundred words a minute, they left the barroom.

Slocum heard one word that he understood in their excited jabbering as they left the saloon. *Grande.*

They returned in a short while. She wore a new unbleached cotton blouse. It had a little lower cut than he thought proper for a young girl, but since she was so poor, it didn't matter. He admired the pleated brown skirt as she swirled it around her ankles above the new sandals. Rafael wore a new shirt of white cloth and new sandals too.

She put the change on the table and mumbled *"Gracias."* Rafael looked around, and then he stepped up and put a silver dollar down beside it.

"The burros were cheap, no?"

"Good," Slocum said, and told them to take chairs by the wall until he finished his business. They quickly obeyed.

The boy was obviously unable to sit, and came over again in a minute. "Does your pinto horse need water and taken out of the sun?"

"That would be fine," Slocum agreed, and watched the boy run off to care for his mount. He turned and nodded at Maria. She smiled, a little easier than the first time, to show him that all was fine. She tugged at her skirt to appear proper for him, and straightened her back. Damn, what tales did she have to tell? He settled in and alternated between puffing on his cigar and sipping the fiery juice.

Jose Morales was one of those handsome Mexican men. Not tall, but lean and hard. His rich smile set Slocum at ease. When Slocum rose to shake the smaller man's hard hand, he knew this was the one. A callused palm indicated he was a worker. Slocum thought Jose had an honest face, and his eyes hid nothing shifty.

The deal was soon consummated. Jose would bring his wife and family by oxen cart and they would be at the ranch in a week.

"Do you have any horses?" Slocum asked.

"Oh, yes, but I would not bring them to her ranch." Jose looked shocked because most gringos did not like the stunted horses of Mexico.

"How many?"

"Six."

"Bring them. There are no horses up there. You will

need them and the ox as well." Slocum was pleased. He considered the horse deal a good one. Even wiry mustangs could herd stock. At least her *vaquero* would be mounted.

"You must come to my *casa*," Jose said.

"I have two others."

"That is no problem. We only have tortillas and frijoles."

"Why don't you buy a sack of flour and beans for the trip too," Slocum said, thinking that food might be short for this man. He gave him four dollars for supplies.

"*Gracias,* you are very generous."

"No problem," Slocum said as he rose to his feet.

They had started to leave when Maria cleared her throat and Slocum recalled her on the back bench. He turned and smiled at her. "Come, we are going to Jose's place to eat and spend the night."

They moved through the doors, and he held them open for the girl to catch up and duck under his arm. When the three of them were on the boardwalk, three dusty riders rode up and dismounted. Slocum looked up and down the street for Rafael and the paint horse. Where had he gone?

The riders came around in a ring of large spur rowels. One reached out, grabbed the girl by the arm, and jerked her up against him. She tried to escape his effort to kiss her. Vexed by the man's actions, Slocum stepped in and clubbed him over the head with his pistol. The blow drove the man to his knees and caved in his Chihuahua peak sombrero, which fell around his neck.

"Dammit, can't you see she wants none of you?" he said, eyeing the other two for any sign of resistance. He steered her after Jose, the gun in his other hand ready for any nonsense from them.

The man on the ground rubbed his greasy black hair. He looked around with his diamond eyes ready to burn.

"You want more?" Slocum demanded, looking at the man for his next move.

"No! Yesterday she was a *puta,*" the man mumbled, shaking his head as he rose unsteady to his feet. "How was I to know—"

"Today, she is my daughter."

"I am sorry, *patron*," the man said, and then started after his amigos as he pushed open both bat-wing doors to escape Slocum's further wrath. Still addled, he seemed uncertain about what had hit him as he disappeared.

"Where's Rafael?" Slocum asked, looking around, mildly upset that the boy wasn't there with his horse as he holstered the Colt.

Maria put her middle two fingers in her mouth and issued the shrillest whistle Slocum had ever heard. And from under the shade of some mesquites down the street, the youth came at a run, leading the paint.

"Good job, Maria," he said.

"*Gracias* to you, *patron*, for saving me," she said softly.

"*De nada*. You are welcome, child, very welcome." He hoped that Lucia liked the two orphans as well as he was beginning to. When the boy caught up, he told him of their plans and they all started up the street for Jose's place. His business in Mexico would soon be over.

10

Sunday morning, Slocum had breakfast with Lucia. He had arrived back in Tombstone the night before, so he was up early, arrived at Nellie's beforehand, and waited in the dining room for her to come down. The shocked look on her face put a grin on his, and then her warm smile made the restaurant a lot brighter. It had threatened to rain since daylight. Veils of dry rain had swept by overhead, the drops evaporating before reaching the ground.

"Well," she said, out of breath, as she swept her dress under her to sit down at his table. "Did you find a family for the ranch?"

"Yes, and some more," he said with a shrug as he resumed his seat across from her. Then he explained about Jose Morales and his family and Rafael and the sister.

She leaned forward, appearing anxious to hear each word, and nodded her approval.

"Coffee?" the waiter asked, holding the silver pot in one hand and a linen napkin in his other.

"Yes," Slocum said, and sat back, realizing how much he had missed her beauty and how he enjoyed the excitement in her blue eyes as he explained things.

"When can we go up there?" she asked after he ordered breakfast for the two of them.

"In a week, I suppose. I need to order some lumber from up in the Chiricahuas at the new mill at Turkey Creek. Then get someone to haul supplies up there, and by then Jose will be there. Will two hundred dollars worth of lumber break you?" he asked, concerned.

"No. Order more if we need it."

"I may double it then."

"What will you build?" she asked.

"A nice adobe main house for you, and then add on the shack for Jose and his family to live in."

"How long will all that take?"

"If I can get help, not that long. Wait. These Oriental waiters—I wonder how Nellie hires them." A new idea had come to him. Hell, the Chinese had built the western half of the first transcontinental railroad, so why not her ranch house and outbuildings.

"Nellie's coming right now," she pointed out. "She wanted to see you about Ike anyway."

"So you're Slocum," the gray-haired matronly woman said, inspecting him as he rose for her. "I guess you sent Ike Clanton packing the other night, didn't you? I never allow him in here when he's drunk, but I had to be in Tucson that night on business."

"No problem, ma'am."

"Please sit down, Mr. Slocum. I'm Nellie, not no ma'am. You sit down there and enjoy yourself. Your breakfasts are on me today. And that gal is a mighty fine young lady, even if she has been mistreated. We have certainly enjoyed her company. You are doing another fine thing fixing her ranch for her. Most men wouldn't take the time."

"No problem. Nice to meet you," he said, sharing a smile with Lucia as the woman strode off.

"I better go ask her about that Chinese help," he added. "Sure isn't anyone around here wants work with the mines offering so many jobs."

He rose and went toward the lobby. Nellie was going in to the office door when he hailed her.

"Yes, Mr. Slocum?" She turned and waited.

"I wondered about your help. How do you get it? I mean, you always seem to have plenty of these Chinese working for you. I could use some up there to work on her ranch building and things."

"China Annie, she's the only one to get them from. No one else can hire them, but from her. She runs the whole show. She lives west off Allen Street. Anyone can show you the way."

"She have some skilled laborers?"

"Always."

"Thanks," he said, and went back to join Lucia. Their breakfast had arrived. Their plates of food were on the table; Lucia looked pleased he had returned.

"Did you find out?"

"I have to see China Annie," he said, and put his napkin in his lap. "She's the one makes the deals."

"How many will you hire?"

"Maybe half a dozen when I get the material, so it will go up fast."

"Good," she said, then leaned over her food and dropped her voice to a whisper. "We need to make another inspection trip up there."

"When I get back from ordering the lumber, we'll do that."

"Good," she said, busy cutting her eggs and not looking up at him.

"Is that soon enough?" he asked quietly.

"No," she said, and still did not look up.

"I'm sorry."

"No, you're not, or you'd take me out there today."

"I promised Doc I would watch his new roosters fight

today." Filled with dread, he waited for her reply.

She wrinkled her slender nose at him over the notion of cockfighting, but then smiled with a sigh. "I can wait."

He nodded that he'd heard her. It wasn't a very good arrangement for them to get together privately, with her staying in the hotel, but it was the only proper one. Nellie would never approve of a man other than a husband in a woman's room in her hotel. He didn't need to risk it, though his fond recollection of their powerful tryst on the Navajo blanket was hard to ignore.

"I'll hurry back from the lumber buying," he promised, recalling her shapely bare legs wrapped around him.

"Good. Do you need money for the material?"

"Yes, payment is usually expected."

"I can get a draft on the bank here."

"We'll do that in the morning," he said, busy eating and speculating about her subtle body under the stiff dress.

After their meal, he left her and went to the Chinese section of Tombstone off West Allen. At China Annie's, the door threshold was so low he had to bend to enter. Then he stood up in the too-sweet smoke that filled the room. Some kind of Chinese drug, he figured. Annie was a short, fat woman. He never could recall seeing such an obese Oriental in his life. She looked like a Buddha in a red silk dress with her head wrapped in a red scarf. She was seated on a throne inside the small house.

"You must be Annie," he said, removing his hat and standing before her.

"You the one they call Slocum?" She seemed proud that she knew his name.

"Yes. You've heard of me?"

"I hear you break chair on Ike Clanton's head. Him no damn good sum-bitch. Him cut queues off my boys and rape my Chinese laundry girls."

"Clanton isn't my favorite character either. I want to hire some of your boys to carpenter and build some buildings on a ranch in the Swisshelm Mountains."

"You hire, good. Boys cost one dollar day. They work

much or I fix them, okay? You kick lazy ones in ass too, huh?'' She grinned, showing a few gaps in her teeth.

"As soon as my lumber gets out there, I want to hire six of them.''

"Good, you come see China Annie. She always get good help for you.''

He had promised to take Lucia to supper that evening after they'd finished eating breakfast, so with the day ahead to himself, he hiked back up Allen to the Oriental and waited for Doc to show up.

"He won't be here too soon,'' the barkeep warned. "When he left here last night, him and Big Nose Kate were drunker than usual and arguing like two bulldogs. He's never in a good mood the next day when the two of them get drunk and fight all night.''

"What about his new roosters?'' Slocum refilled his glass from the bottle he'd bought earlier. "He thinks they're tough.''

"Ah, hell, watch out. There's always folks got better ones. Some of them bring real man-killers to this deal.''

"So it won't be a hands-down deal that Doc wins it all?'' Slocum asked after lighting a cigar to savor. He still held some regrets over leaving Lucia's company to take in some rooster fights with Doc instead.

"Lord, no!''

"Good, I enjoy real competition from time to time.''

"Be plenty of it down there behind the Bird Cage after lunch.''

Slocum checked the clock above the bar. It was ten-thirty. He looked surprised as the tall shoulders and black frock coat of Wyatt Earp darkened the front doors and the man pushed inside. Earp let his hard eyes adjust to the darker interior of the quiet barroom. Then he nodded to Slocum before he went to the bar. He looked up and down as if expecting to see someone else.

"You seen Doc?'' Earp asked the bartender, who was polishing glass.

"Nope. Join the welcoming committee. Slocum's looking for him too." He tossed his head in Slocum's direction.

"You got business with Doc?" Earp turned to Slocum and set his elbows on the bar.

"He and I discussed rooster fighting today," Slocum said, waving to the empty seat beside him.

Earp came over and dropped into the seat, but kept a close look at the front door for the longest while. Then, as if the unspoken concern that had held him was over, he swung around to face Slocum.

"You got Doc's horse back, I heard."

"I did."

"Those damn Cowboys." Earp shook his head and checked the door again. "They robbed the stage again last night between here and Benson."

"Any idea who did it?" Slocum asked

"Some of Clanton's bunch, no doubt."

"Can you prove it."

"No, not yet. There were three of them."

"Where did they go?"

"Hell, off in the desert somewhere. I've got a tracker coming. A Mexican that lived with the Apaches."

"Can he track?"

"Mickey Free. You know him?" Earp asked.

"I've scouted with him."

"Then you can ride with us. Pays ten buck a day plus fifty if we get them."

"I really wanted to see Doc's new roosters fight." Slocum didn't appreciate Earp's bossiness. He would hardly consider an entire day with the man pleasant, and it would be worth a lot more than he had offered.

"Hell, you can do that any time. Come on, get your horse. You have a rifle?"

"Yes, down at Nellie Cashman's."

"Get it. Rolland, tell Doc that we were called away on business."

Slocum wasn't certain that he wanted to ride with the high-handed Earp brother. But nonetheless, he agreed to get his horse and rifle and meet Wyatt in front of the Oriental in ten minutes.

Lucia had gone to church, he learned from the clerk when he managed to get back to the hotel for his armaments. The desk attendant told him she had gone to the Presbyterian church. He went outside and led the paint horse up Fourth Street. Earp was already mounted, and the familiar rider on the roan pony was Mickey Free. His head was wrapped in a red kerchief, and his clothes were tattered and ragged. Just like the last time Slocum had seen him, he still needed a bath. No one ever rode upwind of him.

"Gawdamn!" Free shouted, and then wheeled the roan pony around. "Long damn time since I see you, Slocum."

"Long time. You doing all right?" Slocum looked around to see if there were any others going along.

"Good," Free said.

"It's just the three of us," Earp said, answering his unasked question. "Come on, let's ride. We're only after three of them."

They rode west and past the road to Charleston. On the grade before they reached the Mormon farming community along the San Pedro, Wyatt pointed out the prints to Mickey. The breed dismounted and knelt down to study the tracks, then jumped on his pony and headed southwest, looking at the ground as he rode.

Wyatt handed Slocum a cigar and dismounted. He bit off the end of his and spat it out, and then waited to borrow a lucifer from Slocum.

"That sum-bitch Mickey Free probably caused the biggest Injun fracas in this country when he was a boy, they tell me. You know the story?" Earp tossed his head after the scout who'd ridden off down toward the river tree line. "Oh, hell, he'll find their tracks and be back. You know the whole story about him?"

"Some shave-tail lieutenant got lots of folks killed," Slocum said, recalling the story he had heard many times riding with General Crook. "They say that Mickey's mother moved in with some white man down south of here. I don't think she married him.''

"This West Pointer tried to arrest Cochise?'' Earp squinted his blue eyes as if pained by the notion.

"Yes. He thought Cochise had kidnapped Mickey. But he hadn't, and his people hadn't. A band of Yavapias had kidnapped the boy. Anyway, under a white flag where Ft. Bowie is now, this officer got Cochise in a tent and then arrested him. Cochise escaped through the side of the tent with a knife. But the officer held several of his relatives prisoner in the tent. The lieutenant thought he was big stuff, but before it was over, the Apaches killed the stage line folks at the springs there in revenge, and then slaughtered an entire wagon train of folks going through Apache Pass. The army lost several soldiers from that command in the standoff too. In the end, without orders, the lieutenant hung six male members of Cochise's family in retaliation and then rode back off down here.''

"And they wonder why we've got Apaches wars.'' Wyatt took the cigar out of his mouth and shook his head.

"The government won't ever learn about Indians because they don't want to. Mickey was traded around in other tribes, finally to some Apaches, and ended up in Mexico. One day he simply walked out of the Apache camp and lived among the Mexican people down there. In time, he came back to Arizona. His mother was dead. The head of the scouts, Al Sieber, liked him and hired him to scout. That what I know.''

"Gawdamn, I wish he'd take a bath,'' Earp said, mounting up. "Just once. He stinks worse than a rotted pile of shit. That's why I let him get ahead of us.''

"He must not be able to smell,'' Slocum said, mounting up. That had to be the man's problem.

"I'd even buy the damned soap if he'd bathe,'' Earp said, and put spurs to his big thoroughbred stallion. They rode in silence down to the river, crossed the knee-deep water, and then started up the far bank as thunder rolled across the land.

"Going to get wet on us.'' Earp stopped and sat sideways in his saddle as his horse shook off the river water. "You've got a slicker, I see. So have I, so we won't melt. Maybe it'll bathe that dirty sum-bitch some."

"I've seen him wet before. He don't smell better," Slocum said as he nudged the paint on after Mickey Free, who was out of sight ahead. Still, he smelted remnants of Free's stench above the sweet grass and creosote perfume of the greasewood that rode the fresh wind.

An hour later, they met Mickey squatted in his knee-high boots at the familiar canyon in the base of the Whetstones. Big dark clouds were gathering near the peaks, and the distant rumble of thunder told them the rain was close. Slocum had undone his oilskin slicker, hoping the previous owner had been his size or larger. It fit.

"How many rode up there?" Earp asked Free with a head toss at the mountain.

"Six."

"You sure there was six rode up there?" Wyatt asked.

"Six rode up the canyon." Mickey shrugged his shoulders and then looked at the ground as if it held some interest as he waited for the man's orders.

"Three held up the stage. What do you make of this six business?" Wyatt asked Slocum as they let their horses breathe.

"Ike come to collect his part," Slocum said, wondering when the rain would arrive. "They shared half with him when they robbed from me. I got them to admit it."

"You're serious, aren't you. Why, if I catch that little chicken shit bastard up there, I'd love that. Come on. Let's ride. This storm will hide the sounds of our animals." Wyatt put his foot in the stirrup and on the second try, he mounted. He swung the stud around and smiled for the first time Slocum could ever recall.

"Ike Clanton better have his funeral bills paid," Wyatt said, and motioned for Mickey to go ahead. "You know the way up to their camp?" he asked, turning back.

"It's above the springs up in the junipers, or it was." Slocum motioned toward the rain-shrouded range as he buttoned up the slicker. "But they may post a guard since

I came up here and took their horses, their tack and gear, and all the money they had on them for what they stole off me.''

"Them tracks," Earp said. "Ike must have brought them some more horses."

Slocum looked up at the mountains and wondered if Ike was up there with the three robbers. Someone had resupplied them with guns and horses. The raindrops began to pelt the riders as Earp hurriedly put on his oilskin coat and they rode up the rocky trail after Mickey and his roan.

The next hour there were short, hard showers that drummed on the oilcloth, and then, when the rain quit, the cold wind shifted to hot air again, only to be followed by another wall of hard precipitation.

Slocum glanced back down at the grassy basin streaked with rainstorms below them. The raindrops on his face were cold as ice even though a few minutes before he'd been too hot in the slicker. The first trip he had made up there had been slow so he would not be discovered. This one, covered by the storm's noise and force, found their horses straining on the steep grades, their iron shoes clattering over the wet chert as they hurriedly pushed up single file into the source of the rain.

The stream had become more than just a rivulet, and was belching muddy water as they climbed the last hundred yards to its source. Earp drew out his Winchester. Next he turned and exchanged a nod with Slocum. They were close.

Slocum held up the paint to draw his own rifle out, hoping their ammunition was not damp and would fire. He still had the Colt under his raingear, but wet ammunition many times misfired or didn't fire at all.

Earp drew up his stud, then sent Mickey ahead on foot. Huddled on their horses, the two of them waited for the scout's report as more thunder sounded in the sky above them. A fresh force of wind whipped at them, and a flood ran off Slocum's heavy hat brim like a gutter.

Mickey returned and moved between the two horses to tell them what he'd found.

"Only four of them up there," He held up four brown fingers that glistened with wetness. A flood ran down his face, and the red rag on his head was plastered on his round head. The one-piece faded red underwear he wore was dark with water, as were his too-big ragged canvas pants held up by one suspender strap. The stench was no better either. Slocum tried not to breathe through his nose, but he could taste it anyway, so it made no difference.

"Where's the other two?" Earp asked with a concerned frown.

"Four is all there is," Mickey insisted, and then gave a shrug of his shoulders.

"Fine, you go to the right. And Gawdamnit, Free, don't you shoot Slocum or me."

"I won't." With that the scout went scurrying off around the juniper.

"We better do this on foot," Earp said, looking peeved at the turn of events. "Bet that damn Ike's already gone," he said, and waved Slocum after him.

"I won't bet with you," Slocum said on his heels, doubting Earp heard him as they circled around through the junipers to reach the camp.

The storm increased, and finally Earp shook his head as if anxious to get it over with. He stepped out from behind the tree and took aim at the first one of the outlaws huddled under a canvas shelter stretched between poles by ropes. As if on cue, at Earp's first shot, Mickey's gun blazed from the right, and the confused outlaws struggled to go for their weapons. But it was too late as the pair cut them down in a decisive cross fire. The freckled-faced youth ran out with his hands in the air screaming for them to quit.

"Where's Ike Clanton?" Wyatt raged at him as Slocum and the scout disarmed the downed outlaws in case any were alive. Slocum doubted any had survived.

Wyatt had the boy's shirt in his fist, shaking him like he was a rag doll.

The boy was in tears. "He's not here. Not here, I swear. He left before it started to rain. I swear."

"You rob the stage?"

"No."

"Don't lie to me, boy. You were there last night when they robbed her, weren't you." He had the youth's face close to his. The Smith and Wesson muzzle in his other hand was pressed under the boy's eye.

"Yes, I was there."

"Them others too?"

"Yes. But I only held their horses in the wash."

"But Gawdamnnit, you held it up, didn't you?"

"Yes," the boy cried.

"You've done it before, haven't you." Earp roared above the thunder.

"Not often."

"How many? A dozen times?"

"No! No, not that many times!"

"You're a damn worthless stage robber, aren't you."

"Yes!"

With that settled, Earp threw him on the ground like a rag. The boy remained crouched in a ball, sobbing in his hands, huddled and pleading. Slocum started to turn away in disgust from the pitiful sight. Then, frozen in place, he watched as Earp pointed his handgun down and shot the kid in the back of the head at point-blank range. Life wilted out of the thin body as the boy rolled on his side, his legs straightened and trembled, and he was still. Then a stronger storm swept the camp, jerking the canvas shelter loose from its pinnings and trailing ropes and whipping it away. The sheet struck a juniper top like a sail. Wind tore it loose from the boughs and stripped it up over the tree's top, and Slocum last saw it flapping away in the ensuing storm.

"Damn stage robbers anyway. Only way to handle them. Then they won't get out of prison and do it again," Earp said, standing beside Slocum as they both fought to stand up in the strong gale force of the driving rain.

"The others are dead," Slocum said when the worse of the storm had passed them.

"Good. It's just a damn shame that blasted Ike wasn't here. The breed can bury them. We can ride back now this is settled." Earp went over and talked to Free. He came back and nodded to Slocum that the burial part was settled. Then they both sloshed back in silence to their horses. Slocum mounted up and followed the broad-shouldered Earp down the trail as the rain settled into a lighter soaking with distant rumbles. From time to time as they descended the range, he could even see, between storms in the south, the brooding Huachucha Mountains.

He wished he had stayed in Tombstone for the bloody rooster fights. They would have been mild compared to his day in the Whetstones with Wyatt.

11

"Damnit! The damn rain canceled the cockfights!" Doc said, obviously feeling his whiskey as he crossed the Oriental barroom with a drink in his hand to meet Slocum. "Sah, you look like a man seen a ghost." He batted his blue eyes in a question, and then rocked on his boot heels as he blocked Slocum's way to the bar. Doc's suspenders were down and his tie was undone. This was unusual. Normally he looked like a well-dressed Southern gentleman.

"You've been with Wyatt today?" Doc nodded as if he understood what was wrong and didn't need an answer to his question. He turned on his heels and led Slocum to the bar. "Bring this man a bottle. He needs it."

"I can afford it." Slocum said, not wanting Doc to pay for it.

"Blood money." Doc looked him over from head to toe. Then Doc spoke under his breath as he paid for the bottle and set it and the glass before Slocum. "I should have warned you. Wells Fargo only pays for body counts. They hate robbers. They hate anyone who intends to interrupt their business. You so much as plan a robbery and they want you off the face of this earth forever. That's the man's job.''

Slocum nodded and poured his glass full. He had a lot of drinking to do. Doc set his elbows on the bar and looked over the crowd in the barroom.

"I have the best damn roosters in this cockeyed place and ain't a man in here willing to bet a hundred dollars that he can beat one of mine, is there?'' No answer.

Doc turned back and then downed a half glass of whiskey. Slocum matched it with his own.

''Ah, a race,'' Doc said, and refilled both glasses, sloshing liquor on the bar. He set the bottle down and then they hoisted their glasses. The whiskey soon eased Slocum's pain and made the whole day dissolve into a cloud of care-free splendor. He could no longer see Earp's Smith and Wesson blaze fire out of the barrel not inches from the boy's wet scalp, or feel the acrid smoke from the blast burn his nose. Nor was the twitching of the boy's thin legs straightening and trembling in the arms of death very clear anymore.

"You have to walk some,'' she said. ''I can't carry you two blocks.''

Where was he? And for God sakes, who was she? It was night. Slocum knew that much. He was somewhere outside the Oriental with his arm wrapped over this woman's shoulder. The night air had cooled with the passing of the rain and he felt chilled. There was goose flesh on his arm. His biggest problem was fighting passing out. He was forced to stop her and try to clear his head. He mused to himself that the next time he would feel her tit when he had his arm over her shoulder. He'd do that.

Man, he was drunk. He recalled matching Doc drink for drink, but hell, Doc must be under the table by this time.

"Dot, I mean Doc. Did he pass out?'' Yes, old Holliday, he must have passed out. They had drunk a tub full of whiskey. My God, gallons. She stopped in the middle of the street, and he blinked, unsure where they were. Then she started on again, half carrying him.

"No, not Doc Holliday," she said. "He was singing in the bar when they carried you out to me."

"They carried me out to you?" He couldn't figure anything out. Was she a whore from the Oriental? Not the little girl who wanted to sit on his lap. No, she was a taller woman. Hell, he couldn't tell shit.

"This is the place," she announced, and took a key from her dress pocket to undo the padlock.

"Whose place?" he asked. The vines on the trellis hit his face and he fought them futilely with one hand.

"Kate loaned it to me."

Oh, that was it. She worked for Big Nose Kate. Good, she was one of her girls. She reached in his vest pocket and took out a couple of matches.

"Stay here," she said, leaving him propped up by the door.

"Stay here," he said, lolling the back of his head on the stucco wall. Damn, she was a bossy one. She'd probably take all his money and be gone in the morning. Did he care? Hell, no. But tonight, she better be good in bed or else. She pulled him inside the room and closed the door. A candle was lighted on the table, and he tried to stand up and see it.

"How much did you have to drink?" she asked, stripping off his vest.

"I forgot—I-I better sit on the bed," he said in a small voice. His head was swirling again like he was riding inside a tornado. He had been in a helluva storm—they'd damn sure shot up the damn camp when they'd killed those outlaws.

"That wind whipped . . . that Gawdamn wagon sheet away like a piece of paper," he mumbled as she pulled off his boots.

"What wagon sheet?" she asked.

"Where we were—today." Damn, he kept passing out.

"I have no idea where you were today."

"Oh, hell, I'm not telling you a thing." She didn't need to know—not about that. Worse than some Apache atrocities he'd seen—that bad. His vision swarmed as she undid his pants. He felt her hand close around his manhood and he cried out loud.

"Quiet," she said in his ear. "Or the neighbors will hear us."

"But damn, I'm drunk." He tried to clear his head on the pillow by shaking it.

"I know." She laughed at him. "Are you too drunk to do anything?"

"Why, hell, no. You get them clothes off, girl, and I'll show you."

"I will." He could hear her taunting laughter and he could see glimpses of her undressing in the small flickering candlelight.

Oh, she was beautiful. His vision darkened. Next he awoke and saw the dark rosettes of her nipples in his face as she climbed in the bed. His rough hand felt out of place on her smooth skin as she crowded close to him.

He tried to raise up, his half-hard root in his hand as he was intent on entering her. Then her nimble fingers took it from him and began to restore more life to the shaft. His heart began to pound, and his hips ached to press to hers. She guided him inside her velvet tunnel, and he recalled pumping it to her. And then the world went black.

He awoke. Sunlight was streaming in the small window above them.

It was morning and his head pounded like a cannon. Discovering his hand rested on her silky skin, he drew it back and blinked in shock. The *puta*—no, the woman who'd brought him there was Lucia. He looked under the covers at her subtle spine and bare, shapely butt beside him.

"Are you awake?" she asked sleepily, and rolled over to face him. Her firm breasts were shaking and swinging with her efforts. The brown tips, he remembered—it had been her.

He closed his eyes. What had he told her? He'd been so drunk. Damn, how had she arranged this place for them? He looked around at the mud-stick-waddle ceiling and the plastered walls.

Her warm breath was on his cheek, her groping hand waking up his sleeping force as she gently tugged on it. The long sweet hair was in his face as his fingers closed on her hard butt and her hot tongue teased his ear.

"You have to finish what you started," she said.

"Started?" he asked, and closed his eyes. He wanted to forget the entire past twenty-four hours.

"Yes," she whispered as she moved on top of him, dragging her pear-hard breasts over the swirls of hair on his chest and squirming to put herself on top in a position to receive him.

His root planted inside her, she pushed herself up and grinned down at him. "Who was Colinda?"

"Colinda?" he asked in disbelief. He couldn't think of any Colinda as she began to work up and down his pole. Who cared about her anyway as he raised his head up and at the same time bent her over to taste one of her rock-hard nipples. The sugar flowed into his mouth as he sipped on her sweetness.

"Don't get bucked off," he finally said, out of breath, ready to enjoy her ride.

He pushed and raised his pelvis to meet her attack. She pounded his chest with the sides of her fist as she rode his force. Her head thrown back, she cried for more as they became wilder and wilder until he grew inside her beyond normal proportions. Frantic for more, she urged him on until he exploded, and then they both collapsed into a pile on the cot.

Colinda? He slipped off into a troubled head-splitting nap, his flank sticky with their juices and her body's softness nestled on top of his chest in spent exhaustion. He couldn't remember who Colinda was as he fell into a deeper chasm of sleep.

12

Dawn came over the distant Chiricahuas as he rode out of the still-slumbering Tombstone on the paint. A slinking coyote raised his head to observe him and his mount as they short-loped out of the dry wash and up the hill side on the Gleason Road. Somewhere off in the grass and greasewood brush a topknot quail gave its *whit-whew* whistle. The coyote decided to find cover, and loped off toward the shadowy maroon Dragoons that sat like a great brooding ship above the basin.

Purple doves dusting in the road rose like shots at his approach. The paint's easy lope carried him toward the settlement of Gleason. There he planned to swing east across the Sulphur Spring Valley. It would be dark before he reached Turkey Creek Canyon and the sawmill. He only hoped that they would sell him enough lumber for her needs. The mines were big customers and they had enough money to buy whatever they wanted, usually the entire output of an operation like that sawmill.

A storekeeper in a white apron nodded to him as he held the paint to a walk through Gleason. Doc's woman, Kate, had found Lucia the small house to rent. He wondered if she might regret their arrangement some day when he had to ride on, but he had warned her.

"Slo-cum!" someone called to him.

He reined up the paint and swung him around. He narrowed his eyes to see the man better.

"You and that damn Wyatt have gone into cahoots?" Ike demanded, stepping off the porch of the frame house. Dressed only in his pants and red union suit, he wore a gun. His galluses were down and his rumpled hair was uncombed as he spread his run-down boots apart.

"That's none of your damn business," Slocum said.

"By damn, I'm making it mine. You sums-a-bitches can't kill my men and get by with it."

"They call it stage robbing where I come from," Slocum said. He tried to figure who else besides the worried-faced woman chewing her white knuckles on the porch was with Ike.

"You had a lot of nerve, first stealing them boys' horses and then taking Earp back to kill them." Ike advanced from the yard. His pig eyes were slits. He finally halted fifty feet from Slocum.

"They said you got half of it," Slocum declared.

"They never said nothing like that."

"I'd say you were lucky that Earp didn't get there an hour earlier when you were in camp. He don't take prisoners."

"That sum-bitch is a dead man." Ike spat droplets of spit that shone like diamonds in the sunlight to punctuate his threat.

"Ike, don't reach for that gun of yours. Twice now you've looked like you itched to jerk it out. I'm not warning you, I'm telling you. If you want to be planted here, you go ahead and do it again."

"Ike!" the woman shouted, upset.

"Yes?" Ike never looked at her. His glare was set on Slocum.

"He's a killer, Ike. Don't mess with him," she warned, sounding shaken by the turn of events. "Wait. Your boys will be here soon."

He waved her away with his other hand and turned his attention back to Slocum. "You know you've signed your own death warrant joining them damn Earps?"

"Ike, I won't have to kill you because someone else will save me the effort." His talking over, Slocum turned the paint and started on. The hair on the back of his neck rose. If Ike shot him, it was liable to be in the back, but he had to get on. Nothing that they argued about in the street would settle anything.

"Slocum, I won't need no help to kill you!" Ike shouted after him.

"Go to hell!" Slocum raised his eyes to the mines on the hills above the town. He stood up in the stirrups and then set the horse into a trot. From here on, he needed eyes in the back of his head. Ike would no doubt send some of his men to ambush him. The rage in the man's face and voice was clue enough to his next actions. Damn. Slocum set the paint into a long lope, and when he finally glanced back, his vision of the small community was swallowed by the hills he traveled through.

At noon he stopped in the valley at a Mormon's farm to water his horse. The fresh-planted spindly cottonwoods rustled in the wind in the yard around the unpainted frame shack.

"Mind if I water my horse?" he asked the pregnant young woman who came to the doorway.

"No, sir, help yourself," she said, sweeping back the long brown curls from her face. The wind pressed the thin dress around the swollen ball in front of her narrow hips. Two young children dared peek out from beside her skirt.

"Name's Gunner," she said, squinting against the high sun.

"Nice to meet you, Mrs. Gunner," he said, tipping his hat as his horse took deep droughts of the clear tank. "Sure appreciate the water for paint here."

"Guess we've got plenty. You passing through, huh?"

"Yes, ma'am."

"We don't get many visitors here."

"I reckon not. Kind of off the road." The paint raised his head and let the water slobber from his mouth, then went back for more.

"Ain't no big news, is there?" she asked.

"None I've heard."

"We never hear much out here. Except those renegade Apaches come through here all the time," she said. "I thought they were all on the reservation, but they ain't." In her hand, she grasped her long hair on her shoulder and twisted it.

"They bother you much?"

"Oh, they steal some melons and eat a few sheep. I guess they consider it rent, huh?" She moved a pestering toddler aside with her knee, making a perturbed face at him and then smiling when she looked up again.

"Probably," Slocum said. "I kinda figured they had them on a head count up at San Carlos."

"They can't be counting all of them. They sure pass by here a lot." She looked off toward the purple Chiricahuas.

"Your man around?" Slocum asked, wondering if he might exchange a few words with him.

"Nope." She wrinkled her nose. "He's gone to put up Sister Wanda's alfalfa. You could come in, but the kids, they'd talk, huh?" She wrinkled her nose in helplessness and then smiled openly at him.

"Maybe another time," he said. Then he mounted up and reined the horse around to face her.

"I'll have this young'un by late summer," she said warily, looking down at her stomach. "When he's out, it would be less crowded then, huh?" She winked mischievously at him.

"It might be at that." He nodded as if considering the possibility.

"You come through this way again, you stop and water your horse any time. Can't tell the condition you'll find me in, huh?"

"I'll do that, Mrs. Gunner." He touched his hat to leave.

"Naomia's my name." She swiftly came from the doorway, put her long fingers around his upper leg, and with her thumb squeezed it. Her brown eyes looked up into his as she held him. "You come back again, mister. It gets pretty damn lonely in this place."

"I will," he said as he lifted the reins and backed the horse away. She followed a few steps.

'I'm not bad-looking when I ain't pregnant," she shouted to him.

"You aren't bad-looking that way," he said, and then sent the paint on his way. "But I've got business to tend to."

"I never heard your name!" she shouted, hurrying after him with her skirt in her hands.

"Slocum."

"Good! Slocum, you come back and see me." she said after him, and waved to him as the pair of toddlers caught up with her.

13

The Turkey Creek sawmill and yard bustled with activity in the late afternoon shadows as he rode up. Logs were being skidded along by several teamsters. A strong smell of pitch hung in the air, along with smoke spiralling upward from the boiler. The whine of a great-toothed saw slicing out boards screamed on the canyon wind. Slocum dismounted in front of an official-looking shed.

"Evening," a lanky man said, coming out the front door. His clothing was generously spiced with fresh sawdust. "Can I help you?"

"I'm needing to buy some lumber. They told me there was a chance you'd sell me some."

"A chance is right. You aren't a millwright, are you?"

Slocum shook his head. "Never ran a saw in my life."

"Shame. I could sure use another hand. How much you need and where?" The man extended his hand with an introduction. "Jay Stevens. This is my operation, if the Apaches don't come back and burn me out."

"Most of them are gone. Nice to meet you. Slocum's mine. See, this lady I work for has this ranch in the Swisshelms. Wants a house pattern and some for roofs on the rest of her outbuildings." Slocum fished out his paper with the dimensions needed and handed it to the man.

"We probably have that in the yard." Stevens bobbed his head as if considering the matter as settled. "But you're going to have to find you a hauler. We could sell a lot more if we could find more freighters. There isn't anyone wants to haul lumber when they can make big money hauling ore to the crusher."

"Where can I find one?"

"There's an Arkie, Billy Ray Martin, lives south of here, with some mules. He does some hauling."

"How come he isn't hauling ore?"

"He's establishing a ranch. He may be hard to hire."

"I'll ride out and see him in the morning. Be all right to camp here?"

"Sure, come on up to the cookshack. The wife has supper ready. We're about to shut down for the day."

"I don't want to impose," Slocum said, offering the man a way out.

"No problem. She's use to everyone falling in at mealtime." Stevens smiled warmly and brushed the sawdust off the front of his shirt. Finally, seeing it was hopeless, he led the way toward the raw lumber buildings.

Slocum put the paint in a corral, washed up, and joined the crew for their evening meal at a long table. Stevens's wife was an attractive woman in her thirties, and aided by two older Mexican women, she soon had the long table bristling with steaming bowls of beans, potatoes and beef. The mill hands nodded in greeting to Slocum, and soon were fully absorbed in filling their plates.

"Manners may lack a little here, Mr. Slocum," she said, reaching past him to place a platter of fresh-sliced white bread on the table. "I'm Nelda Stevens. Don't bother to stand. Nice to have you here."

"Yes, ma'am," he said after her as she hurried off directing her helpers to other details.

"You in the mining business?" a red-whiskered mill hand asked on his right.

"Ranching right now," Slocum said, completing his plate and passing on the gravy boat.

"Rustlers are bad up here," the man said, then wadded a half a slice of bread in his mouth.

"There's cures for that."

The man nodded. "But they have a big gang."

"You're talking about the Cowboys?"

The man paused, then looked up around as if checking to be certain there was no one overhearing them. "I mean Ike Clanton and his bunch. Yeah, they call them the Cowboys."

"You tangled with them?"

"They shot my brother in the back."

Slocum frowned at the man's words. "What for?"

"Ten dollars and his hat, I guess."

"That's not much. What kind of hat?"

"A Boss of the Plains Stetson."

"Your brother a cowboy?"

The man's head nodded, and between forks of food he managed, "He worked for Henry Iverson."

"Where's this Iverson at?"

"Dead too, I guess. Ain't no one seen him in months."

"I'll heed your words. I've had a run-in or two with Ike." Slocum cut the tender strips of roast beef.

"You met Billy Clanton yet?"

"No."

"He's the one I figure killed Buck."

"He hangs out a lot in Mexico, got a whore down there," the older man on the other side said. "Watch him, he's a backshooter. Ain't he, Rupe."

"Red ain't a-jawing none about that Billy being a backshooter," the older man on the far side said. "That whole bunch has run roughshod over everyone in this county."

"Maybe their time is about over?" Slocum asked between bites.

"Not as long as Johnny Behan is the law." Rupe lowered his voice guardedly. "He's in with them."

"What about the Earps?"

"No way, they'd never be elected. They're all Republicans. They could do it, but the vote would be for a yellow dog as long as he's a Democrat. No, Behan will be the sheriff forever, I guess. He kinda holds with them."

"You understand that federal law supersedes territory law."

"I know, but don't count Behan out. He's a real politician. Made thirty thousand dollars last year collecting fines and taxes, so he ain't about to piss on the fire and call in the dogs, not yet, mister."

Slocum agreed with a nod and went on eating. On top of all his other problems, he had to find a lumber hauler and that might be the biggest challenge yet.

He saddled his horse at first light to ride for the freighter's place. He looked up to see Nelda Stevens coming with something in her hands.

"Can't you stay for breakfast?" she asked.

"I need to ride on, ma'am." The girth tight, he dropped the stirrup down and turned to face the woman.

"Then take this hot bread." She placed the cloth-wrapped biscuits in his hand. For a long moment he expected her to say more, but she gently dismissed him with shake of her head. Lips compressed tight, she turned her gaze to the mountains.

He thanked her, then mounted up, hearing her warning to ride carefully. Her present was still hot, and the heat from it warmed his hand. He touched his hat to salute the tall slender woman before he rode south. Filled with a new urgency, he wanted to make a deal on the hauling as quickly as possible, then get back and be sure Lucia was all right. His choosing sides in the Clanton-Earp war might not be the best for her safety.

He short-loped the paint on the wagon road out of Turkey Creek. The night before, he'd paid for the lumber after supper. The freighter's place was about five miles down the canyon and to the left, according to Stevens's directions. Slocum managed to ride out of the live oaks a few hours later into an open meadow, and spotted the log cabin and the fresh new shingle roof.

"Hold it right there!" a man in overalls ordered from the doorway. A shock of black dark as a raven's wing was on his head. He held a Winchester at his waist leveled at Slocum.

"I'm a friend. Stevens sent me from the sawmill."

"I ain't taking no chances. Ride up here close-like and tell me your name."

"Slocum. I need some lumber hauled down in the Swisshelms for my boss."

"Billy Ray Martin, mister, is my name. You sure you ain't a damn Lowery or Clanton?" The man looked hard at him for an answer.

"We have a common enemy sounds like."

"All right, put your hands down, but I swear if you're one of them . . ."

Slocum dismounted and hitched the paint to the rear wagon wheel. He saw the big sorrel mules in the corral as he turned back.

"My boss needs the lumber I bought delivered to the Swisshelms."

"Ain't hardly got time to haul freight." Martin shook his head in despair. "They're always after me to haul some. I took a few loads to Paradise last week in exchange for barn lumber." The man set the long gun inside the door and then invited him in.

"You didn't hear of a man called McClain there, did you?" Slocum asked.

"He rides for them Clantons?"

"Yes, I think he does."

"Yeah, I heard of him. He's dying of lead poisoning, they say, from a charge of buckshot to his guts. Some whore named Sarah, I think, is nursing him."

"That's my boss's ex-husband."

"She was married to him?" He blinked his dark eyes in disbelief.

"He lied to her family about starting a ranch, then spent

the money they sent for stock. Joined up with Ike is the way I've got the story."

"Them jaspers tried to steal my mules after they come by here all friendly-like, but they was only checking me out." Martin indicated a chair for him at the table, then took a rag as a hot-holder and hefted the granite coffeepot off the stove.

"How did you stop them from taking your mules?" Slocum wanted to hear Martin's story.

"By jingoes, I taught them mules to kick hell out of anyone tried to mess with them but me before I left Yell County."

"Good idea."

"I done heard stories about Injuns stealing a man's stock as well as yellow-bellies like that Clanton bunch. So I taught Jude and Willy that they better kick up their old heels."

"They look like good mules," he said, nodding thanks for the cup of steaming brew.

"Best they are."

"How much you going to charge me?"

"If I haul it, you mean?"

"Yes, how much?"

"A keg of sixteen-penny nails for the first trip. I ain't real good on money figuring, but I need them nails to put up the barn I plan to put up. After the first trip I'll know how long it takes to get there."

"I'll have a keg at the ranch when you get there."

"Take me two days, no, three, and I should be there."

"You take the military road south and where the small creek comes out of the Swisshelms, there's a dim wagon road into the ranch."

"Her name's McClain?"

"Yes. See you there in three days."

Slocum rose and shook the man's leathery hand. He guessed him to be in his mid-twenties. Lanky but with a powerful way, he looked like a man not unused to hard work. Slocum wouldn't broach the matter yet, but he might be the man for her. She would need a foreman, and whatever Billy Ray didn't know about ranching, he could learn from the Mexicans.

They shook hands on the deal, and Slocum planned to leave. It would be past dark when he returned to Tombstone if he rode hard. Outside, he reset the girth on his saddle, mounted up, and thanked his host for the coffee and their agreement. He had miles to cover.

The Sulphur Spring Valley was a wide basin with only a few clusters of cottonwoods that lined the center along the intermittent stream. He was trotting the horse standing in the stirrup, heading across the greening grassland for the south end of the hulking Dragoons, when the shot rang out. The paint faltered between his knees, and he barely had time to kick his boots out of the stirrups before the horse's nose touched the ground.

Two more shots whined close by his ear as he sprawled face-down in the stiff dead grass. How many were shooting at him? His six-gun in his fist, he could hear the moan of the dying horse close by lying on its side. He gritted his teeth over the loss. His enemies were after him. How many and where were they? He moved around on his belly, not anxious to expose himself to some potshot that might hit the mark. They had aimed to hit him, and the bullet had come in low and to the right and struck the paint instead.

The shooter was north of him. Ike had sicced one of his dogs on him, and he'd waited on the trail knowing that Slocum was likely to ride out of the Chiricahuas and go back to Tombstone. Being too predictable had been the cause of this. The paint's thrashing and moans beside him drew some hard swear words from his dry lips. He needed to get to where he could put him out of his misery.

The blast of his .44 echoed across the wide expanse around them. *There. No more pain, old paint.*

14

It was past dark. A sudden late afternoon thundershower had drenched him by the time he reached the Mormon woman's place. A dog barked at his approach and he paused by the corral. Lightning illuminated the yard and pens. There were only the same horses inside them that he had seen the day before.

"Someone out there?" she called from the dark doorway. Then a flash of distant lightning showed her wearing a full-length white cotton gown, her long dark hair down.

"Shut up, Joe," she scolded the dog. "Who's out there?"

"It's me, Naomia. Slocum."

"My gosh, man, where is your horse?"

"Someone shot him out from under me. Has anyone rode by here in the past few hours?"

"No. My lands, have you had any supper? You're soaking wet."

"That's the least of my worries. I need to buy or borrow a horse."

"Come inside. The children are asleep and I have some food left. His few clothes here won't fit you." She shook her head at the impossibility. "You're a lot taller than he is. You can take a minute to eat. My lands, you'll take a death of cold and this rain has set in." She closed the door behind him; the rains drummed on the roof. Far off the roll of the storm's thunder carried across the basin.

With his belly growling at his backbone and his only food since morning the three biscuits, he could hardly refuse her hospitality. She lighted a candle on the table and set about fixing him a plate.

"Your husband still putting up hay?" he asked, taking a seat.

She turned and nodded at him. "That's his other wife. You understand?"

"Oh," he said, realizing he wasn't only putting up hay at Sister Wanda's. The man was a polygamist—lots of them in the Southwest.

When she brought the plate over, he could see in the flickering light the dollar-size dark circles under the thin material of her shift.

"I'm not ugly, am I?" she asked, holding the plate above his place.

"Heavens, no." His words were drowned out by the roar of more thunder.

"Good," she said, nodding her head. Then, after setting the plate down, she began combing her long dark hair back with her fingers. "A woman living out here alone a lot can wonder about a lot of things. You eat and I'll talk. I may sound like a madwoman, but I don't have anyone to talk to."

He saw her chew on her lower lip as if in doubt about continuing. To make her at ease, he began eating. The rain's patter on the roof grew louder, and more thunder joined the melee outside.

"See, we got married and took our honeymoon coming here from Utah. That was five years ago. I had Joseph nine months later. He's coming four. The Apaches were coming by then often, and I prayed to God every night that they didn't take him or kill us.

"I lost my second one about seven months along. She's buried under the cottonwoods. Then I had Amsworth. He'll soon be a year. Apaches killed Wanda's husband when they broke out of San Carlos. She and her man come here from Utah too." Then diamond-size tears began to flood her eyelids as the flashes outside increased.

"The church told him to marry her since she was a widow. Wanda's pretty, her breasts aren't like mine. Nursing my first one ruined mine for good. You know what I mean?"

He frowned at her. They looked nice to him under the shift. She was like lots of woman stranded on some outlying ranch—very lonely and insecure.

"I'll show you," she said, raising up from her chair opposite him. In an instant, she had gathered up the hem and lifted the garment to her chin, exposing her rounded stomach and both breasts.

"See, this one is long," she said, holding it up as she came around for his examination. "And this one is rock hard. Feel it."

His hand cupped the fuller one as she pressed it toward him. It was hard as a rock. Then she placed his other hand on the left one. It was subtle and thinner.

"See what I mean? Wanda has small pointed ones." She began to sniffle, holding his hands tightly in place on them. "Now he only comes to spend a night when I'm not pregnant."

"He doesn't come help you?" He rose to his feet, feeling a rising in his pants.

"He only comes in the daytime. Then he has to go back to her."

He nodded that he understood, and she closed her eyes tight as he raised up to kiss her. Her mouth became a hungry shark and moved all over his, despite the two-day stubble around his lips. Her hands sought his gunbelt buckle, quickly undid it, and placed the holster on the table.

Then she tore at his fly, her fingertips fumbling and racing to open his damp pants.

She paused to allow him to hoist the gown off over her head and toss it aside. Quickly she peeled the jeans off his hips. Her exploring palm rubbed over the underwear that encased his bulging privates.

"Oh, God, help me!" she cried at her discovery. "I'm shaking. Look at me."

"You'll be fine. Here, let me take off my boots," he whispered, feeling handicapped by the combination of footwear, pants at his knees, and the damp one-piece underwear he still wore.

"I'll help you over there." She giggled with excitement.

Holding up his britches, he shuffled to the iron-poster bed. When he was seated, she wrestled off his soaked boots and socks, then folded his pants over a chair in haste as he undid his shirt buttons. The storm's beating on the roof grew louder, and wind whistled at the corners of the small house.

In an instant, she was straddling him, undoing his underwear and stripping it off his shoulders. Then, like a ravenous animal, she sunk her sharp teeth into the bare skin of his shoulder as she fought the garment down. His hand slipped between her legs, and he began to probe her hot wetness. She bit harder as she quickly scooted forward, encircled his throbbing root with her finger, and then thrust herself on his spear.

Her cry was so loud, he feared she would awaken the two children.

"I want under you," she said, breathless.

He agreed. The bed protested as they switched positions. On top of her, he spread her legs open. Impatient for him to be in her, she pulled him down on top. Her stomach separated them in the middle, but it didn't encumber her movements, nor did it slow her craving for all he had to offer. Around them, the fury of the storm threatened the very walls and roof as they sought each other. Deeper and deeper he plunged as she raised her hips to meet him. Great roars rolled above them, and lightning made the room like daylight as they fought the sea of passion.

Ropes strung beneath the thin mattress moaned in protest. Their fury matched the violence outside. Then, finally, they collided pelvis to pelvis, and a great gasp of relief escaped her throat as he made the final surge and then held hard in place.

Out of breath, they fell in a heap side by side as the storm left to the southwest. A cold drop of rain splattered on his bare chest.

"Oh, damn, we've got to move the bed," she said. "I've told him for six months to fix that roof. He hasn't done a thing about it."

They both rose up and managed with one on each end to scoot it closer to the table. Then, with her arms folded over her bare breasts, she inspected the underside of the shingles for more leaks. With a shake of her head, she hurried over and found a kettle to place on the dirt floor.

The resounding bings of many droplets in the pan made a musical sound. He sat on a chair and tried to clear his head. It had turned out to be quite a day since he'd left the sawmill. He'd hired Billy Ray Martin to haul the lumber, he'd lost the paint horse to some backshooter who he'd heard ride off afterwards, been caught in a storm, made love to a neglected pregnant woman, and he still lacked a half day's ride of getting back to Tombstone. Things in his life were in a mess as usual. The main thing in his craw was that he owed Ike Clanton at least a pistol-whipping for sending someone out to try to kill him. Maybe Doc Holliday was right. The only way to settle with a rattler was cut his head off.

"May I sit in your lap?" she asked in a quiet little girl's voice, standing before him. She was still nude, and the long tresses of her hair covered her breasts. The candlelight flickered on the small ball of her stomach as she waited for his reply.

"Sure, come here," he said, opening his arms for her. Then he leaned over and blew out the candle flame. Somewhere in the south, the faint roll of thunder drummed back down the Sulphur Spring Valley as she nestled her head on his shoulder and he hugged her tight. *No, you're not ugly or crazy, Naomia.*

15

The topknot quail scurried across the road in the purple pre-dawn light. Slocum kept to the shadows, not entering Gleason from the east, but riding in from the south, in case Ike had set up a sentry. He reined up the borrowed horse on the rise. Through a veil of mesquites, he could see the white-painted frame house where Ike had stood on the porch when he had ridden through. Dismounted, he hitched the horse to a chicken pen of prickly occatilla stakes. He undid the thong on the Colt's hammer, and then he drew the long Bowie knife from his belt sheath. If Ike was home, he was going to be surprised by an early morning visitor.

He kept close to the store building wall, then paused for his breath and heart rate to catch up. Ignoring the cowardly town curs that barked at everything, he checked the shadowy street. Squinting to determine if any guard was about, but seeing nothing out of place, he quickly crossed the street on his boot heels. His ears straining to hear, he edged around the dwelling, stepping around several bunches of pancake cactus planted no doubt for ornament in a land where lawns would only waste precious water.

Satisfied the window beside him led to a bedroom, he used his blade to pry the frame up. There was a small protesting sound of dry wood against wood, and he paused and waited. Then, satisfied the noise was slight, he continued to steadily lift the pane.

Two forms slept under the covers on the bed. The one close to Slocum, emitting the loud snores, was obviously Ike. On the bedpost hung his six-gun. Slocum stepped over and removed it from the holster.

Then Ike stopped breathing. Slocum froze in place, ready to shove the handgun in his belt. Seconds thundered by, with nothing but the steady breathing of the woman on the other side. Then, in a shuddering snort, Ike began to saw away again. Slocum relaxed as the cooler air from the window filled the room.

"Ike, who opened that window?" the woman said, sitting up, clutching the sheet to her.

"I opened it," Slocum said in a dry low voice.

A piercing scream escaped her throat. Tearing the cover from Ike, she raced for the door shrieking at the top of her lungs. While the sheet covered her front, her ample ass was bare as she fought to get the door open, yelling at the top of her lungs for help. Finally it came open, and she staggered away into the hallway gathering the trailing sheet in her haste.

Ike rolled over and blindly grappled for his gun, fighting himself awake until he felt the steel of Slocum's knife blade laid against his throat. He choked off his cursing, and except for the woman's panicky screaming outside in the street, there was no sound to be heard, just Ike's breathing through his nose like a raging fire as he froze in place.

"Don't kill me," he gasped.

"It all depends on you," Slocum said, pressing the keen edge a little deeper.

"You want money?"

"Did you send that backshooter after me?"

"No."

Slocum grasped a handful of his greasy hair to pull him upright, then drew the knife deeper into Ike's throat. "Don't lie to me."

"Okay, I did. You shouldn't have joined them Earps."

"Listen!" Slocum raised the outlaw up from the bed by his hair. "You are never going to know when I'll be back. You try to bushwhack me again, I won't wake you to cut your throat wide open, Ike."

"I understand—for God's sake don't kill me," Ike screamed as Slocum sliced off his hair below his fist and let the babbling Ike fall back in the bed. A stream of urine arched in the air as Ike crawfished across the bed on his back to escape Slocum's fury. Ike's hands furiously searched his scalp for any wound as he moaned for mercy. Wide-eyed, he edged to the far side of the bed, then tumbled on the floor in a thud.

Slocum shot a splintering shot at the door frame as Ike passed through it on his hands and knees screaming for help. His broad bare butt went of sight as he scrambled like a runaway hog for safety.

A six-gun in each hand, Slocum slipped out the window. Somewhere in front of the house, Ike was pleading for anyone to bring him a gun. Slocum could see his backside from the corner of his house—so far no one had come to the man's aid.

"Bring me a gun! I'll kill the bastard!"

Slocum jumped the small yard fence. The pot-bellied naked Ike waved his arms like a windmill until he whirled and then froze at the sight of Slocum. Two quick shots in the dust at his feet sent the bare-ass outlaw diving for his life into the front yard.

"Gawddamn cactus!" Ike shrieked as he landed belly down on a large bed of prickly pear. "Oh, hell, I'm ruined for life!"

Slocum's lips formed a grim smile as he reached the

horse. Maybe Ike would think the next time before he sent one of his rannies after him again. Mounted, he turned the horse toward Tombstone. In the distance, he could see sun shining on those buildings atop the next mesa.

16

He dismounted at Pasco's stable. He found the owner inside huddled over his desk and a pile of papers.

"I need someone to return a horse for me," Slocum announced.

"Damn people in Hell are wanting ice water. What else do you want, Slocum?" Pasco's bloodshot eyes told the whole story; he was hung over.

"It goes back to Mrs. Gunner in Sulphur Springs Valley."

"There's two of them."

"Naomia Gunner," Slocum said as he put two dollars down on the desk. "Take care of it for me."

"I suppose I can. Behan and the coroner are going up in the Whetstones. They say there are some dead men buried up there."

"What's that got to do with me?" If they had found the dead stage robbers, they couldn't prove a thing to implicate him.

"Hell, it was the front-page story on the *Epitaph*. Figured you needed in on the latest news since you've been gone for two days. Oh, yeah, last night, Big Nose Kate whipped hell out of two miners in the center of Allen Street. They tore the front of her dress off her before it was over. You know, a bare-breasted woman throwing punches is damn exciting. They could have sold tickets. I think them two got to watching her tits instead of her fists."

"I need a saddle too. You sell the ones I brought in?"

"Got the best one left. What happened to your paint?"

"Fell in a gopher hole, had to shoot him and walk to Gunner's place."

"Damn!" Pasco frowned as if he had not heard him right. "Did it rain over there?"

"Yes. I walked in it. See that her horse gets back to her." Slocum paused in the doorway waiting for confirmation.

"I will." Pasco waved him on his way.

Slocum left him and headed for the small adobe house a block away. He hoped Lucia had made it all right in his absence. Passing several Mexican children rolling a small wheel rim with sticks in noisy competition, he walked downhill toward the heavy wooden front door under the trellis.

"Anyone home?" he shouted as he rapped on the facing.

No answer.

Had she gone shopping? He pulled the latch string and pushed the door inward. It protested on its hinges, and he warily searched around the room. The bed was made, the dishes all done on the dry sink. There were dead insects floating in the water pail. Obviously she had not been there in some time.

Then he saw a note on the table. He read it slowly, his heartbeat quickening as a ball formed in his empty stomach.

Slocum
You want to see her again alive, you get a thousand
dollars.

Damn. He crushed the note in his fist. He headed out the
door with his head down. They had taken her and wanted
more ransom than he could raise robbing every bank in
Tombstone. Was Ike Clanton behind this? Then why had
he had someone shoot at him out in Sulphur Springs
Valley? It didn't make sense. Maybe Doc Holliday would
have an answer. He headed for the Oriental as fast as
possible.

He barely acknowledged the men he passed on the
street who spoke to him. The very thought that those thugs
had their greedy hands on Lucia was enough to make him
grind his molars. He slammed through the bat-wing doors
and saw the drawn face of Holliday turn from his place
at the bar.

"Why, my word, my good man, where have you
been?" he asked.

"They took her," he said, looking for the bartender. A
good round of whiskey might settle him down so he could
think.

"Took who?"

"Mrs. McClain. They kidnapped her while I was gone.
They left a damn note telling me to get a thousand dollars
ransom."

"Is that all?" Doc asked, turning back to the bar. He
hoisted his glass and drank deeply. Then he coughed into
a clean linen kerchief, which he folded, but not before
Slocum saw the fresh blood.

"We can raise that," Doc said, straightening and re-
gaining his composure.

"And pay them?" Slocum was shocked that Doc was
so willing to part with such a large sum of money. Paying
them the money had been his last thought, up until Doc
mentioned it.

"Pay them at all costs," Doc said. "We can't allow
them to harm her, sah."

"I agree, but where do we get a thousand dollars and how do we pay it back?" He waved the barkeep over and ordered some bonded whiskey.

"We of course take it back."

"Oh, sure."

"Trust me. I shall have the money for you in legal tender in twenty-four hours. Then when the lady is safe, we simply go after them and take the money back."

Slocum motioned for the barkeep to leave the bottle. He figured he had a long wait ahead while Doc found the money. Splashing liquor in the empty glass before him, he wondered how well Doc's plan would work.

"There's Virgil now," Doc said, turning and resting his elbows on the bar.

"Slocum, Doc, have you heard? They just brought Ike Clanton into the Doc's. Something about him diving stark naked into a bed of prickly pear." Virgil chuckled to himself. "Wished I'd seen that."

"Was he drunk?" Doc asked.

"Word is some guy got him out of bed and chased him around the house shooting at him. It was jump in the cactus or get his butt shot off."

"Why, his pecker must be full of them spines."

"That, and the rest of him. Behan was down there sucking up to him, asking him who done it. Ike won't say except he was going to get him."

"He won't have to look far," Slocum said, and then downed his first glass of whiskey.

"You do that?" Earp asked.

"That's what I can't figure out." Slocum pointed to the nude painting behind the bar. The buxom gal's right breast was larger than the left one. Not as bad a mismatch as poor Naomia's, but still . . . He'd never wondered about that before.

"We got more problem than Ike's pecker being full of spines. Someone's kidnapped Mrs. McClain," Doc said.

"Besides that, one of Ike's men tried to bushwhack me out in the Sulphur Springs Valley," Slocum said. "They shot the paint out from under me instead."

"He's really after you," Virgil said, shaking his head. "Sorry you got mixed up in our business. Who took her?"

"We don't know. They left a ransom note. Slocum, that shooting at you did two things," Doc said pointedly. "It made you late getting back, so they had more time to get away with her. And it made you not suspect those damn Cowboys, because they need you to get the ransom."

"Son of a bitch. Where have they got Ike?" Slocum slapped his glass on the bar.

"Easy, son, let Ike fester. You've done him lots of good already today. Right, Virgil?"

"Yes, and I'll go with you and we'll talk to folks around her place. Someone saw them ride off and knows who took her."

"Good." Slocum agreed. A lawman along might be the key to learning all about her abductors. "Save the bottle, I'll be back," he shouted to the barkeep.

"And I, sah, will have the necessary money drawn up to redeem her," Doc said, clapping him on the shoulder. "Don't you worry none. She's as good as returned."

"Thanks," he said, and followed the lawman out the front doors. He only wished he shared Doc's confidence. They had meant to kill his horse after all. He wished he was a fly on the wall when that doctor extracted those thorns out of Ike's private parts. It wasn't a bad enough punishment for taking Lucia hostage.

17

"Curly Bill's coming, Marshal Earp!" A flush-faced boy, out of breath, came at the dead run to where Slocum and Virgil were talking to Mrs. Gutterez.

"Calm down, boy. Get your breath. Bill's been here before."

"They sent word. This time he's really on the prowl."

"Let that old tomcat prowl. If he comes to Tombstone looking for a belly full of buckshot, I'll oblige him." Virgil gave the boy a dime and turned back to talk with the woman. "Now you said two men came and got Mrs. McClain?" Virgil asked her.

"*Sí*, they said that the señor here had been hurt. A load of lumber had fell on him at the ranch." The woman indicated Slocum. So he knew how they drew her out of town.

"What did these two look like?" Slocum asked the woman.

"Gringo cowboys. One they call the Kid. He had the

pimples on his face.'' She shrugged her thick shoulders and looked at Earp as if she knew no more.

"Thanks," the tall man said to excuse her.

"Two of Ike's boys," Slocum said. He knew the pair that she had meant. He had seen them in the Swisshelms riding with Ike. Lucia had not seen their faces that day so she didn't know to avoid them.

"Where have they taken her?" Virgil asked after they both thanked the woman. She had turned with a shrug and gone inside her house.

"She wasn't up in his house in Gleason. I was there this morning."

"Old Man Clanton has a ranch across the San Pedro ten miles from here down at Charleston."

"I guess I better go check it out," Slocum said as they hiked up the hard-packed street.

"Hold up." Virgil caught his sleeve. "That ain't like his house at Gleason with Mrs. Wright. This place is an armed camp. You can't tell how many gunmen are up there. You go riding in and you'll get your ass shot off."

"I understand, Virgil. I still intend to check it out."

At Fremont Street, he shook Virgil's hand and thanked him for the help. Then he set out for the livery halfway down the block for a fresh horse and directions to the Clanton Ranch.

"You can't miss it," Pasco said, chewing on a straw and leaning against the office door facing. "Cross the Charleston bridge and it sits on that ridge about a mile east of the town."

"Good," Slocum said, cinching up his latest saddle. It was not a bad one and it fit the bay horse's withers all right. Many rigs were built on too narrow a tree, and soon had a mount saddle sore. This model had a deep enough gullet, and the sheepskin lining was still intact. Piled on top of two Navajo pads, it should suffice. He finished lacing the latigos tight and turned to Pasco.

"Keep my comings and goings under your hat?"

"I don't owe them bastards nothing. Besides, they all stable over at the OK Corral."

"Good. You thinking about tying one on tonight?"

Pasco shook his head no and made a disgusted face at him. "You get back we'll throw a real one."

"A real one," Slocum agreed, and reined the horse around and out the big open gate onto Fremont Street. He rode past the city hall, Fly's Photographic Studio, Doc and Kate's bungalow, and the Earps' house. He set his heels to the bay to make him trot, and stood up in the stirrups. The bay trotted past the boot hill cemetery, a series of crosses and some stones in the tall dead grass that went over the hillside on the right. Slocum planned to make Charleston by dark. Just right for his purposes. He studied the distant towering Whetstone Mountains far to the west. The Clanton gang would regret messing with Lucia when he was through with them.

He arrived in Charleston after sundown. Buffalo soldiers from nearby Ft. Huachucha were spilling out of a small cantina for blacks only. Someone was playing a banjo on a bench, and two privates were doing a jig in the street.

"Howdy there, sir," a tall sergeant said, saluting Slocum as he rode up.

"Evening. It must be payday," he said, drawing up the bay to let him breathe before he crossed the bridge and rode into the main part of town.

"Aw, yes, but we be having fun all the time."

"No Apache trouble?"

"Aw, yes, sir, there still be some, but we done sat on our butts for two months at them water holes, so we rejoicing here tonight."

"Good, have fun."

"Sergeant Hill! She be ready for you now!" someone called out from the doorway.

"I best be going in there." The non-com grinned from ear to ear in the twilight. The catcalls of the others cheered him on as they slapped his arms and offered to take his place while he hurried up through the pack of well-wishers to the lighted door.

"They only got two whores working here," a private

said to inform Slocum. "And rank done got its privilege, sir."

"I recall. You have fun, boys," he said, and lifted the reins and waved as he rode on. The music never stopped, and a few more enlisted men were outside dancing by the time he reached the bridge.

His horse's hooves drummed over the bridge. He could hear the stamp mill crushing the ore. The efforts shook the ground. This was the railhead for Tombstone, and the great ore wagons were parked in no order as he rode past them. He paused in front of the Lady Luck Saloon, hitched his horse, and parted the bat-wing doors to enter the smoky interior.

"What'll it be?" the barmaid shouted over the tinny piano and a dozen raucous voices singing in the corner.

"Beer and a meal."

"Corned beef and hash?"

"That the best you have?"

"It ain't bad," she said, her palms flat on the table, leaning far enough forward he could see down the front of her blouse to the brown nipples.

"I'll take it."

"You want some company? We got some new girls." She tossed her head in the direction of the bar. On cue, a young brunette raised her dress halfway up her shapely calf for his inspection while flashing an inviting smile.

He shook his head no. This was no pleasure trip. He had business to take care of. Somewhere east of there was the Clantons' main headquarters and possibly the place where they held Lucia. To go in like an Indian might be what they were waiting for. He might need to go in like a drunk who belonged there. He planned to scout the barroom crowds for someone from the ranch and follow them in. There was bound to be at least one of the gang members in town lapping up booze. All he needed was a lead on one. He'd handle it from there.

Past eleven o'clock, in the Double Eagle Saloon, he found Shorty Stauffer, an employee of Old Man Clanton. Stauffer was a bowlegged waddy who talked with a lisp, and drinking didn't improve his speech. "I thay" was how he started most of his speeches.

"I say, I worked for the old man going on two years. Him down in Mexico now, though. He sent some of the boys down there to gather cattle, and the damn Mexicans stole the cattle back from them. Made him so damn mad he sent Billy and Finn down there to get them back. They come back with a few."

"Here, have some more whiskey." Slocum refilled his glass. "What happened next?"

"I thought the old man would make me go down there, but he took some of the other hands and went off to Arido and set up shop. I say, the damn beef business is too damn good not to have a good supply of it coming for the slaughterhouses up here."

"Right. Let's drink to good beef prices." Slocum raised his glass to toast with Shorty.

"I say, you are a real buddy. You ride up to Kansas ever?" Shorty asked.

"Sure, I was there."

"I knowed you from somewhere. Did I seen you in Dodge once?" Shorty's eyes were rheumy and he had a hard time sitting up as he raised his glass.

"Drink to Dodge," Slocum said, waving his glass in front of the weaving cowboy.

"I screwed a good—one there—once." Shorty fell face-down on the table. "She was something," he babbled on the tabletop.

"I better take you back to the ranch. Ike out there?"

"Ike who?" Shorty asked as Slocum slipped his arms under his shoulders and hoisted him to his feet.

"Ike Clanton. Is he at the ranch?"

"Naw, he's pumping that—Mrs Wright's butt—up there at Gleason and the old man comes home—oh, I say, there will be hell to pay over that." Shorty made a moaning sound as Slocum hustled him out into the night.

"Where's your horse?"

"He's a damn bay sum-bitch. Right there."

"I'll tighten the cinch."

"Good. I ever tell you about the dunk, I mean the drunk cowboy—oh, that's me. Come out of the bar one night got on his horse backwards. Reached over and found the horse's tail for its mane and he thought someone had cut his pony's head off. So he put his thumb in the horse's jugular vein to save him bleeding to death and rode him home like that." Shorty slapped both knees as he broke up laughing. "Thought his head was cut off."

"You that drunk?" Slocum asked as he helped the cowboy in the saddle.

"I say, no. But I am a little drunk."

"Hell, you work hard, you deserve a little drunk."

"Damn right."

"You want me to ride a ways with you?"

"I'll be fine." Shorty swayed around, barely catching the horn to hold his seat.

"I'll just tag along so you don't fall out and break your head open."

"I say—Joe, you are a good—one. I say, you ought to work with us."

"I might, if you'd introduce me to the boss."

"Finn might hire you. Come along."

"I'll do that, pard," Slocum said, and swung up on his own horse. Things were going according to plan. He didn't know Finn, so he could suppose the man didn't know him, and if Ike was still picking out cactus thorns at wherever—he was going to ride in on the Clanton ranch.

Somewhere off in the night a coyote gave a mournful call. Then another answered, and their lonely wails carried up and down the San Pedro River, a silver stream in the moonlight below the two men as they rode eastward for the Clanton ranch.

18

"That you, Shorty?" a voice called from out in the night. Slocum knew the time was at hand. They had guards posted at the perimeter of the ranch—the first place he had to get by.

"Hell, yes, it's me," the cowboy slurred as he weaved in the saddle.

"Who's that with you?"

By then Slocum could see the armed man ride out in the starlight. He carried a rifle. There was no cover around them, save for the dark willows along the river at the base of the hill to Slocum's left. His hand rested close to the grip on his .44. The darkness might hide a lot and it might not. He listened for Shorty's explanation.

"New man, Joe Spain."

"I knew a Spain once in Texas." The guard rode in closer.

"Around San Saba?" Slocum asked.

"Yeah, his name was—"

"Walter Spain. He was my brother." The man was bearded and burly. Slocum held his place, watching in the pearly light for any hostile move by the man. He knew that Walter Spain had swung on a hemp rope. Taken from the San Saba jail one night by irate citizens for his butchery of some whore with a skinning knife.

"They hung him there," the man said, trying to see Slocum better. The rifle was held ready in his arms.

"He got a tough deal," Slocum said.

"Anybody got hung had a tough deal. Finn never mentioned no new man, but I knew your brother. You're half as tough as he was, we can use you."

Slocum touched his hat to the man and booted his horse to catch up with Shorty. As he drew alongside, the puncher was singing some ditty.

"There once was this lady from Shash who had such a terrible rash. Oh, no one would pay her cash, to poke his thing up her stash."

Then Shorty yodeled a chorus to the stars. "There was nothing doctors could be do for her condition, so she flew away in a different direction, where no one was wise to her affliction."

More of his yodeling followed the second verse. "Now the sailors at sea scratch at the rash, gained from the lady from Stash, who lives by the sea and is spending their cash."

Slocum turned in the saddle, placing the position of the guard as best he could do by the hulking black shape of the Huachuchas, in case he had to flee suddenly from the ranch. The dark river bottoms might be too choked with salt willows to try to head into them on horseback in the dark.

"Spain, that was Luke Black on guard. He's a good old boy. You see, he's just doing his job." Then Shorty began muttering to himself.

"I understand perfectly. You can't be careful enough."

"You see, the damn Mexicans shot three of our boys."

"How come?"

"They wanted their damn cattle back, I guess." Shorty

chuckled and then went to coughing. Finally he straightened. "You see, we evened it on them, though. By God, we went down there and raped all their women and young girls. Curly Bill even cut the ears off their mayor in this one small village. Showed them greasers, didn't we?"

"I guess," Slocum said. "You must have a war going on down there."

"Naw, the old man's moved down there to show them how powerful we are. They ain't tried much since either. Old Man Clanton is a mean sum-bitch." Shorty reined up at the corral. "We made it."

Where would they hold her? Slocum dropped from the saddle. Except for one lit lamp in a main house window, the rest of the place was dark.

"We can put our saddles on the fence. It damn sure— not going to—ain't going to rain," Shorty mumbled, staggering about as he tried to undo his latigos. Slocum finally did it for him, swinging the rig up beside his own. As his eyes grew more accustomed to the starlight, he could see there wasn't much to the ranch; horse pens, a low-roofed adobe at the side that he figured was the tack shed, and a sprawling main house.

"Bunks—this way," Shorty said with a wave of his arm. "You can meet Finn in the morning. He's 'sleep by now."

Slocum's next mission was to get Shorty asleep so he could search the house, and he only had a few hours to do it all. Then, he had to hope the others remained asleep while he located Lucia. Time was short. He needed to be long gone by the time the ranch woke up. He could only hope they hadn't taken her to Mexico where the old man was at.

"That you, Shorty?" some sleepy-voiced hand asked as they clunked into the dark bunk room attached to the main house. The room stank of horse, sweaty socks, and tobacco as Slocum tried to orient himself.

"It ain't no big-titted whore from El Paso!" Shorty said out loud.

A chorus of "Shut up!" came from the various two-story beds along the walls. By Slocum's count, there were a half dozen or more men in the room. He wished Shorty would close his mouth and climb in his rack. He needed to locate Lucia McClain and then whisk her away. The clock was ticking away. He had less than an hour before daylight by his own estimation. Damn, he hoped they hadn't hurt her. They'd pay dearly if they'd harmed a single hair on her head.

19

Slocum eased his frame from the top bed. He had taken
the bunk Shorty had pointed out as being empty. As he
lowered himself down from the top, the snoozing of the
man in the lower rack paused, and then the man flopped
over to face the wall. With the man's sleep resumed, Slocum began breathing again. His gunbelt slung over his
shoulder, he carefully crossed the room without kicking
over anything, and reached the door he hoped entered the
main part of the house.

With no idea of the layout or who was under the roof
besides the gang members in the bunk room, he began his
search for her. Shorty had mentioned that Ike's other
brother was in charge with the old man in Mexico. Where
did he sleep? Slocum stepped out into a dark hallway.
Only some starlight coming in a window at the other end
gave him even a glimmer of light. He eased the door shut
to the bunk room, and waited until his breathing was
slowed before he continued.

Each boot step on the gritty floor sounded like a rock being crushed. The first door on the right was closed. He tried the knob, and the latch released. Steadily, he opened the door until he could see where the starlight streamed in the window onto a white sheet. Belly down in his one-piece underwear, a man lay across the mattress. Obviously she wasn't in there. He quickly shut the door and then moved down the hall. Pausing at the next closed door, he again tried the knob. The protest of the latch sounded like a shrieking cat as he gritted his teeth and stopped. What next?

He still held the round handle in his grip. Seconds ticked by, and the back of his neck itched. Nothing happened. He continued his twist, and the door finally came open. The room smelled of saddle leather oil and the sulphurous aroma of gunpowder. Like a cat he slipped inside. With no window to let in any light, he knew what he had to do. Carefully he struck a lucifer on the facing and held the light high for a quick survey. The room had several cases of explosives and some harness on the rack behind him. Old Man Clanton sure had enough explosives to blow half the territory to hell and gone. He quickly doused the light, and for a moment was blinded by the total darkness.

Turning his ear toward the core of the building, he listened. No sounds in the hall. He went back out to continue his search. Where was she? How many more rooms were left? He eased down the corridor step by step. Nothing in the next room, but furniture. His heart pounded in his throat. How much time did he have left to search for her?

In the main room, he tried to look to the east out of the window and see if dawn was close. The darkness in that direction satisfied him that he still had time to look further. He dried his palms on the front of his pants. Which way should he search next? There was a kitchen. Maybe a room led off it and they kept her there. He could see pots and pans hanging down from the rafters. Were there more rooms beyond—

"Don't move!" Something hard and sharp poked him

in the back and he froze in his tracks. What now? Slowly
he raised his hands over his head. This bunch by reputation was trigger happy. He had only a moment to figure
a way out because his life hung on a thin thread.

20

"Damn cowboys, you get in my kitchen. I catchy you red-handed!" Obviously the Chinese cook of the Clanton outfit was behind him holding a meat cleaver to his back.

"Hell, I missed supper last night getting here," Slocum said and whirled around, wrestling the cleaver away from the shorter man in the dark room.

"Oh, I see you new cowboy. Someone steal all my damn raisins. You not one do that?"

"Hell, no! I just got here. Where they got that McClain woman at?"

"Who woman? No know about her. She come last night with you?"

"No. The McClain woman they kidnapped. They say she's a looker. I want to see her. What room is she in?"

"Lee Wong no know about no woman here." He shook his head vehemently. "Me fix you food quickee, got to start breakfast. Boys be up in hour."

Good. That settled it. Lucia wasn't there and her kid-

127

napping wasn't common knowledge at the Clanton headquarters. The cook knew everything that went on in a
place like this. More than likely it was one of Ike's own
schemes, and he didn't intend to cut the others in or didn't
trust them to know about it. Slocum planned to have that
meal Wong offered him, and then about fifteen minutes
before good light to ride out across the San Pedro.

When the kitchen lamps were lighted, Slocum took a
seat and watched Wong stoke the big stove, the queue
swinging around the small man's head. Wong quickly had
down a quarter side of beef, slicing off several thin slices.
He waited for Slocum's approval.

"That's fine."

While the skillet heated, white flour flew as the cook
made bread as quickly as anyone Slocum had ever seen.
That included some very capable cooks on cattle drives.
His job finished, Wong set a cast-iron skillet on the stove
and went to washing, then slicing the potatoes. The speed
of the little man was impressive. Wherever the Clantons
had found Wong, they had located a handy man for the
job.

"You go to Mexico to help old man?" Wong narrowed
his eyes, and the lamplight heightened the deep yellow of
his skin.

"Whatever they got for me to do." Slocum shrugged
like it made no difference.

"Wong, he no go to Mexico. Me citizen United States.
Maybe Mexico send me back to China." He waved a
spatula around to make his point.

"They might do that. You sure can't trust Mexicans,"
Slocum said as seriously as he could, satisfied that the old
man probably wanted Wong down there. He could see the
reason why as the man stoked the stove and then started
two giant pots of coffee to boil. The heart of an army is
its belly. Old Man Clanton knew that.

Slocum ate the cold biscuits and browned meat. He
even had the first cup of morning coffee. Then he thanked
Wong, ready to take his leave, and asked where the privy
was.

"Outside." Wong pointed to the side door. "What your name?"

"Joe Spain. And thanks."

"You very welcome, Joe Spain, you come back in twenty minutes I feed you good again." He grinned and showed his discolored teeth.

Outside the house, Slocum headed for the corral, caught the bay, saddled him, and rode around the perimeter. He was giving the gelding his head going down the steep hillside toward the dark salt willows that lined the San Pedro when he heard Wong ringing on the triangle for the gang to rise and shine. Somewhere in the east, an orange glow silhouetted the saw-edge mountains. He headed for Tombstone still wondering where they were holding her.

A lonely quail gave a *whit-whew* to his mate off in the brush. Somewhere in the cottonwoods, some mourning doves called as Slocum prepared to ford the shallow stream. He grinned to himself as the gelding gained the far bank and shook hard enough to rattle the stirrups. He bet Shorty and Wong were wondering where Joe Spain had gone. Maybe the night guard had brought it up at breakfast. Where was the new man?

It would all be very funny if he knew where Lucia McClain was being held. He also needed to meet Billy Ray Martin at her ranch with a keg of nails for payment. He'd better get moving. The Morales family was due there any time as well. A rifle and ammo for his ranch help wouldn't be a bad idea either.

He arrived in Tombstone at seven. Doc had already gone home to bed when Slocum checked at the Oriental. He rode over to the stables and roused Pasco out of bed in his office.

"Damn, Slocum, what do you need now?" the man complained, throwing back the covers.

"A packsaddle to go on that cranky Ap horse. I need to take some supplies up to the ranch. You haven't sold him, have you?"

"Why, hell, no, no one wants him. You're the only one

can get anything out of him. Word's out they've kid-napped her. That woman of yours?" Pasco rubbed his stubbled face in his hands as he sat on the edge of the bunk in a state of sullen dejection.

"Yes, they did, but she ain't at Clanton's ranch," Slocum said, then lighted a cigar as he leaned on the door casing and waited for the man.

Pasco whistled in disbelief, then shook his head. "I can hardly believe that you searched Clanton's ranch house and lived to talk about it."

"Hell, I did that and ate breakfast with their cook, Wong."

"What else is going to happen? They're accusing Doc of robbing the Benson stage."

"Who said that?" Things were going to hell in a hand-basket.

"Hell, I guess he beat hell out of Big Nosed Kate and she went running to Behan ready to testify to it."

"What did he beat her for?"

"She probably needed it, knowing her." Pasco put up his galluses as he rose and shook his head in disapproval of the entire matter. "Man gets me up this early should be shot." He held up his hands in defense. "Damn, I'm sorry they got your lady friend all mixed up in this, but it's going to be open war between Doc, them Earps, and the Clanton-Lowery clan before this is all over. You just mark my words." He headed out the door, brushing Slocum aside as he went, grumbling under his breath about "Some people never learn a damn thing."

An hour later, the packhorse was loaded, with a key of sixteen-penny nails, fifty pounds of flour, fifty pounds of dry beans, ten pounds of coffee, some lard, a new Winchester 44-40, and two hundred rounds of ammunition. The Ap switched his tail and impatiently stomped his right hind foot. Mounted, Slocum rode in close and busted him on the butt with a lead shank, and they left Tombstone on the run.

He was past the Gleason Road before he drew both animals down to a trot, and by then the Ap was disoriented enough that he kept up. Slocum planned to be at the ranch by early afternoon. If nothing held him up, he felt certain he could be there close to that time. He rode by several freighters who waved, heading their teams of six oxen hauling double wagons in the direction of Tombstone.

He paused at the head of the canyon with the sun high, to water the horses and let them breathe. The Ap kept stomping his right hoof, so Slocum checked it and found nothing wrong with the frog. Simply another bad habit in an incorrigible animal. He shook his head and fished out some jerky out of his shirt pocket that he had grabbed at the last moment in the mercantile earlier.

A Mexican mockingbird in the live oak scolded him as he sat on the ground cross-legged. He had found no further notes from the kidnappers at her place or the post office. Where were they holding her? He shook his head and gnawed on the dry jerky. *Lucia, I'm looking hard for you, honey.*

21

He rode up the canyon, expecting to round the corner any moment and see the shack and corral. A smile crossed his lips at the sight of Martin's green wagon, and the mules grazing nearby lifted their heads to bray at his horses. Martin, with a fresh board in his hands, was busy unloading.

"I was getting worried this might not be her ranch," he said with a wide grin.

"Any sign of the Morales family?" Slocum asked, dismounting.

"No one here but me and my mules. It looks like it'll take me five trips to get all the lumber you bought up here."

"We can afford to have it hauled. I wonder if Jose has been delayed." Slocum scratched his temple. What else was going to go wrong? The man and his family should have be there. "Martin, you know anything about two of Ike's men, Pepper Bill and Tyler Lee?"

"They hang out at Paradise a lot. Pair of hardcases for sure." Martin shook his head in disgust.

"Can you draw me a map of Paradise?" Slocum asked. Why hadn't he thought of there? Damn, they'd taken her behind the Chiricahuas. That was where Landon McClain was recovering too. Was he mixed up in this business of her kidnapping? Maybe it wasn't lke's plan after all, but their own private one. McClain, Pepper Bill, and Tyler Lee. Damn, he needed to do something.

Who made that whistle? Slocum frowned at the loud sound and looked down the canyon. Riding a thin gray horse, Rafael came bouncing into view, herding a small band of loose horses and burros. On another mount, her smile flashing, Maria waved a brown arm at Slocum.

"Where's Jose?" he asked when they reached him.

"He is coming," Rafael said, sliding off his horse and giving his sister the reins to hold. "Are you proud of us? We drove the horses all the way."

"Yes." Slocum hugged him.

"Where is the señora?" Maria asked, looking around disappointed.

"Some men have kidnapped her."

"You mean the lady that you work for has been taken by them damn Clantons?" Martin asked.

"I think so. The woman next door said that two men who sound like Pepper Bill and Tyler Lee took her away saying I was hurt up here. They left me a note on the table saying I needed to get a thousand dollars ransom."

"Whew, they want a lot for her. I don't mean she ain't worth that much, but I can't count that high."

"Neither can I. Martin, you stay here and get everyone settled in. I can pay you for your time. I'm riding to Paradise and finding her if they have her there."

"No. I need to go with you. I know that place and can help you."

Slocum shook his head.

"The three of you should go find the señora," Maria said. "I will tell Jose where you went and he can start to work on this place. I thought it would be all fixed up."

She wrinkled her small nose in disappointment.

"Some day it will be *grande*," Slocum said, and patted her leg to reassure her. "But Rafael must stay here. These men are dangerous."

"No, señor. He is very clever. He can help search for her while you confuse them, no?"

"My sister knows what I can do," Rafael said, anxious for Slocum's approval.

"All right. What will you ride, Martin?"

"Why, one of my mules, of course."

"It's eighty miles to Paradise from here." Slocum could not believe anyone could ride a draft mule bareback that far.

"Shucks, Slocum, I could ride Willy clear back home to Yell County," Martin drawled.

"We need some food," Slocum said, wondering where they'd get it.

"You have supplies on the horse?" Maria asked.

"Yes."

"Take it inside for me. Then you men make some firewood so I can make tortillas with the flour, and there are frijoles here too. Is there pots?"

"There's a stove inside and a few skillets."

"Go shoot a few blue grouses. I will start the cooking." Skirt in her hands, she ran to the shack.

"Now that girl has got gumption," Martin said with a shake of his head. "I like that in a woman. I'll do it."

"Impressive, isn't she?" Slocum said with a smile. Maria had her first serious admirer in the Arizona Territory.

When the food was taken inside, Slocum mounted his horse and shook loose his lariat to go after wood. Rafael was coming back with an armload of sticks. "We better hurry. She expects things to go fast or she gets mad."

"Yeah, and cute as a kitten and she's sharp too," Martin said as he checked the edge of the ax that Landon McClain had left behind. "This axe is pure dull. I'll have to get my rock from the wagon and work it over. You can't chop firewood with a dull ax."

Slocum used his bay horse to drag in deadwood for

them. He could see Martin could do more with an ax than most men. He already had a stack of split wood rowed up beside the door.

"Coffee!" Maria cried from the doorway. No one needed a second invitation. The three were glad to leave the wood behind, and crowded in around the small table she had cleared for them. She'd used everything for mugs from tin cans to chipped enamel cups.

"No sugar, no milk." She wrinkled her nose at Slocum as she turned snow-white tortillas over in the skillet with her fingers.

"I've got a can of evaporated milk in my wagon," Martin said, and put down his cup to run after it.

"Now all you lack is sugar," Slocum said over his steaming cup, and winked at her.

"Is he married?" she asked in a whisper.

"No. Do you like him?"

She turned quickly away, ignoring his question, and busied herself with the tortillas. The coffee tasted rich. It restored Slocum, but not enough for the ride ahead. He traveled well alone. But with one Arkie and a boy tagging along, he wasn't certain about how it would work. Maybe he should just go alone; he couldn't risk Lucia's life. But Martin did know the lay of the land in Paradise and the boy was a regular ferret.

"Here's that milk, ma'am," Martin said, holding the can out to her as if it were a gift.

"*Gracias, Señor,*" she said, accepting it, holding her slender chin out as elegantly as any queen. "You are very generous, señor."

"Wasn't anything at all."

Slocum thought the man blushed.

"Did anyone shoot a grouse?" she asked.

"Never saw one," Slocum said.

"All you get, then, is beans and tortillas."

"It'll be fine, ma'am," Martin said, and then busied himself with his coffee. "All I was having to eat anyway was some hoecakes I brung along if you all hadn't showed up."

"After we eat, we'll ride as far as Martin's place tonight," Slocum announced. "We can rest a while there, and then head up through Turkey Creek and over the pass into Paradise."

Everyone agreed as Maria rolled hot steaming beans in the blanket tortillas. She held the first one out to Slocum since he was the *patron,* as she called him. He thanked her, but doubted she heard as she gave the starry-eyed Martin his tortilla. Then she gave one to Rafael.

"Will Jose be here tomorrow?" Slocum asked her privately when she came back to the stove.

"Maybe two days. Tomorrow I will go tell him we found the place. Why?"

"There are many outlaws in these mountains all the time. That damn rifle is too big for you." He exhaled through his nose, then put his right boot on top of the chair. He drew out the .22 derringer for her.

"Can you use this?" he asked. She sure needed some protection.

"*Sí.*"

"Don't shoot an amigo."

"I won't," she said with a shudder of her thin shoulders. Then tears began to flow, and he gently hugged her to his chest.

"It will be all right soon, Maria. We will get the señora back and she will have a fine ranch here."

"Oh, *patron,* I knew our prayers were answered when you pistol-whipped that *vaquero* for me. I am no baby, but our parents were killed by those bandits and we were alone. Rafael and I . . ." She began to sob. Then she hurried outside.

"Can I do anything for her?" Martin asked with another of her tortillas in his fist.

"No, she will be fine. It was a long trip and she was disappointed. She expected a hacienda to be here."

"A long ways from that yet," Martin said.

Slocum agreed. *Lucia, we're coming*. He closed his eyes. Nothing was moving fast enough or sure enough to suit him concerning her rescue.

22

Satisfied that Maria could cock and fire the small derringer, he hid the extra rifle under the bed by tying it to the ropes under the mattress, and told her to have Jose use it if necessary. The ammunition he stored in the bottom of an old trunk. Then he piled soiled and ragged clothing on top of the cartons. Slocum straightened, looking around for anything that he had missed.

"Be very careful, Maria, when you ride out to find Jose and his family."

"I will, *patron*, and I will pray to the Virgin Mary that you find the señora safe and bring her back quickly." She rushed over and hugged him like a daughter.

Slocum kissed her on the forehead and then he hurried outside, for the others were mounted and waiting. Martin sat his tall mule, and the boy was on his gray. The quarter moon wasn't up yet, and Slocum wanted more light to make the long ride. But there wasn't time, and they weren't liable to ride off a mountain. He nodded that he was ready. In the saddle, he led the way down the canyon in silence.

He had made many nightime marches through this land with the army pursuing the Apaches into Mexico, but somehow he dreaded this one worse than any other. Guilt nagged at him. Had he done all he could to find Lucia? His notion of revenge against Ike might have complicated things. What if they'd harmed her? He would never forgive himself. If not for him, she would have been safe in Nellie Cashman's hotel and not been in some whore's house waiting for him. He booted the bay into a faster trot.

They rode north as the moon slipped over the brooding mountains to their right. Giant mounds sat like sitting hens, their highest peaks against the sky like the teeth of a red wolf. The lunar light gleamed on the points. He had seen this land with the tall Cochise himself, been in his camp, slept with a woman of his band. One-Who-Counts-Stars had been her name. The guttural syllables in the Apache version of it he could no longer pronounce. She had told him many things about his future—most had come true.

"You are the wind, and like the wind you will never be able to stay in any woman's bed. You must do the things the winds does, move on, blow down the canyon, and scatter the ashes of old campfires. You must carry dust to new lands beyond the last mountains and pollinate the corn," she had told him. Her hard callused palms had caressed his face as her diamond eyes had sparkled in the moonlight only inches from him. Somewhere in the Dragoons, he had left her. It had been supposed to be only for a short while, but he had been gone for a long time. However, when he'd returned, he hadn't been able to find her among the Chiricahuas there. In time, some of the Apaches had told him that she had gone to Mexico, and probably lived in the Sierra Madres with her people who'd remained there.

Later on, he'd ridden scout with General Crook, and when the Gray Wolf had left for Washington the first time, he'd quit the service. This land of shadows, sweeping bats, and owls silently gliding by overhead meant much to him, as did the islands of mountains that were scattered about on this sea of grass. He fought the tiredness and leaden eyelids as he rode on. The others were coming with him. He could hear their mounts' footfalls. Uncomplaining, the pair followed him through the night.

Near dawn, they dropped heavily from their mounts at Martin's cabin. Horses were put up and grained. Then they staggered to the house without a word. Martin fell across his bunk with a groan. Slocum tossed the boy a blanket. Rafael caught it in his arms and then went outside. Then Slocum unfurled his own bedroll and spread it on the floor. In minutes, he was asleep, too tired to care about anything.

Sunlight streamed in the open doorway. Slocum forced open his eyes at the discovery. How long had they slept? He rose, scrubbing the stubble on his face. They needed to move on. He headed outside to empty his bladder and think about what he had to do to get the three of them riding. Beyond the yard area, he finished his business and turned to go back to the house.

"Don't move!" someone ordered. "Hands high."

Slocum whirled to see the big man aboard a dun horse holding a long-barrel Army-model Colt on him. No one in the outlaw business carried a cap and ball pistol unless they knew a lot about them. He raised his hands, wondering who this bearded mountain of a man was.

"Who the hell are you?" Slocum finally asked.

"I'll ask the damn questions, mister. Who the hell are *you*?"

"Name's Slocum."

"Curly Bill Brocious. Why, you're the sum-bitch sent Ike into the damn prickly pear." His mouth opened a red gap in his thick gray-black beard as he laughed out loud. His great frame shook as mirth consumed him. "I can't believe that damn Ike jumped on top of a prickly pear bed. You must be a mean sum-bitch."

"Get going," someone ordered, and Slocum saw another man bring Billy Ray outside with his hands up. Damn, he had hoped Curly Bill was alone. He needed to figure out a way to turn the tables on these two—they weren't there to teach Sunday school.

"Bring him over here, Ringo," Brocious ordered.

"What we going to do with them?" the hatless man in a black frock coat asked.

"I bet Ike would pay two hundred bucks reward for this jasper," Brocious said, swinging his big gut over the fork of the saddle and heavily dismounting.

'What the hell are you talking about?" Ringo asked, blinking his steel-gray eyes that looked a little like he'd taken one too many shots of redeye the night before.

"This is the cactus jumper."

"Jesus, did you do that to poor Ike? I understand he leaks all over when he pees now. Kind of like one those fountains they have in St Louis."

Then Ringo broke out laughing until he lost his breath and had a coughing fit.

"What's so damn funny?" Brocious frowned at his associate.

"We need to ask—" He paused for his breath. "We need to ask Mrs. Wright if he does it fifteen different ways now."

"Shit, Ringo, that ain't even funny." Scowling, he turned back to Slocum and Martin. "You fellas got any money?"

Slocum shook his head. Martin took his lead and did the same.

"We ain't got shit here, Ringo. Search them fellas. I think that red mule will bring maybe fifty bucks, and I've seen that bay around before." Brocious became intent on the horses in the pen. "That gray your packhorse?"

"Yeah, little Mexican horse we use for a packhorse," Slocum said, wondering where Rafael was located. Probably still asleep somewhere out under a juniper. Maybe it would spare the boy getting shot by these two cutthroats.

"That mule broke to ride?" Brocious asked.

"Oh, yes, sir, that mule is a good riding animal," Billy Ray said. "You should try him. You'd like to ride him. A big man like you needs a good mount."

"Yeah? What's wrong with him then?" Brocious asked as Ringo searched their pockets. "You ain't doing me no favors."

"Oh, I just thought we could trade you."

"Trade what?" His broad brows formed a bridge as he scowled at Martin. "Ringo, they got any money on them?"

"I found fifty dollars on Slocum and none on this fella."

"Then you go saddle that mule and ride him."

"Me? Why me? I ain't no damn mule man."

"I want to see someone ride him."

"Saddle him yourself. You're the big horse-breaker," Ringo said, handing the money to him.

"That damn mule is some kinda trick. No one says take my mule, not even a dumb Arkie." He stuffed the currency and coins in his vest pockets, not taking his eyes off the two of them.

The first shot blew dust all over Brocious. He raised his gun high as if to draw back. Ready for the opportunity, Slocum drove a fist in his midsection. Beside him, Billy Ray kicked Ringo in the crotch with his brogan.

A long "ah" sound came from Ringo's mouth as he bent over, holding himself with his handgun, and slowly sank to his knees. Martin moved in. Slocum's haymaker connected with Brocious's jaw and flung the man back. Then two more blows from Slocum's fists sent him spinning. His opponent addled but obviously not through, Slocum took the opportunity and grasped his gun hand. He tried to break the outlaw's forearm on his knee. As a result, the .44 hit the ground, but the action drew a raging shout from Brocious. Then Martin whacked him on the back of the head with a double tree. The big man's eyes swarmed, and then he flopped belly down in the dust.

"Señor, are you all right?" Rafael asked, the Winchester in his hands as he came running.

"I'm fine. You did wonderful."

"You did great, Rafael." Martin said, holding the double tree and looking for any sign of fight in either Ringo, who held his hands high, or the groaning Brocious.

"Get a rope and we'll tie them up," Slocum said. "We haven't time to mess with them." Then Slocum stuck Brocious's own pistol in his face as he took his money back, along with all the man had in his vest pockets. Satisfied he had at least doubled his money, Slocum straightened.

"I should put you on a cactus bed like I did Ike. Only I don't think you are half as slinking a coward as he is."

"Slocum, you stay in this country much longer, I'll nail your hide to the barn wall." Brocious squinted his eyes with the hate burning from them like smoldering coals as he rose to his feet.

"Better save your gunpowder for the others. They say your days are numbered in this country."

"Who's that, them Earps and Holliday?" Brocious shouted as Martin finished tying his hands behind his back.

"What's your excuse, Ringo?" Slocum asked.

"I'm a card man myself. Would you like to draw for high card?"

"But I have all the aces." Slocum began to thrust up his hands behind his back.

"Obviously, sir. Not too tight, my good man. I knew a man lost his hand that was tied too tight for too long. I need mine to deal with, thank you."

"Rafael, get the lariat ropes from their horses," Slocum said.

Without a word, the boy ran to obey orders. When he returned, Slocum forced Brocious to step in the loop, and drew it around his ankles. Then, lariat in hand, he stepped in the man's stirrup, and then seated, he gathered up the rope.

"What the hell you doing?" the big man demanded.

"Hanging you," Slocum said. "I don't expect you to

learn much today, but upside down you may learn a little.''

"You no-good bastard," Brocious shouted as Slocum dallied the rope on the horn, jerked him off his feet, and unceremoniously dragged the big man on the seat of his pants to the base of a large Ponderosa pine. He tossed a second rope over a limb and told the boy to put its loop around Brocious's feet. Ignoring the outlaw's vocal protesting, he drove the pony away, and soon the man's great girth hung with his head only inches off the ground.

"One more word out of you and I'll hang you right side up," Slocum said. His words silenced the outlaw as he swung back and forth. The rope squeaked under the weight as it cut into the limb's bark.

"We doing Ringo the same way?" Martin asked as he secured the second rope to a nearby sapling to hold Brocious off the ground.

"Yes. Maybe they'll realize what a real hanging is like."

"I'll get you, Slocum. This ain't funny," Brocious shouted. "Damn, you can't leave me like this."

"It wasn't meant to be funny," Slocum said as he backed the dun pony and they drew the squalling Ringo up in the next tall pine tree. The wailing gambler was soon tied in his new position.

"All right, boys, gather all the horses and their guns and we ride," Slocum said as Martin finished tying Ringo's rope off.

"Sí, patron," Rafael said, and rushed off.

"You reckon the mail rider will find them about noon when he passes here?" Martin asked.

"He may, but if they don't talk nice to him, he may not cut them down." Slocum shared a grin with the man as Ringo wailed like a baby to be cut down. The sight of the pair gently swinging back and forth in the early morning breeze was enough for Slocum. They had mountains to cross and a woman to rescue. *Lucia, I'm coming.*

23

"That's Paradise," Martin said with a shrug as they let their horses blow. In the late afternoon, the shadows of the Chiricahuas spread over the land and out into the San Pedro Valley beyond. There was nothing down there, Slocum could see, except a handful of false-front buildings and a few larger tent operations, which were either stores, whorehouses, or saloons. Some shacks and individual tents were scattered around them on the juniper-clad hillside.

"We can't go busting in there like lawmen which we aren't, and second, we might get her killed if she's there." Slocum gripped the saddlehorn and stretched his tender back muscles as he considered his options. There weren't many.

"So what do we do?" Martin asked.

"You must let a Mexican boy go learn where she is," Rafael said with a wrinkle of his very Castilian nose.

"Too dangerous," Slocum replied.

"No, it is too dangerous if you go, *patron*. Those men who have her, they know you, no?"

Slocum agreed with a bob of his head. Perhaps the boy had a point. If Rafael could find her undiscovered, then perhaps they could rush in and save her. "The men who have her are called Tyler Lee and Pepper Bill. Here, take my jackknife. You may need it."

"*Gracias.*" Rafael hopped down from his horse and came to collect the knife.

"Don't you stab on one that don't need it," Slocum said before he handed it to the boy.

"I won't. I will meet you back here later tonight."

"Be careful."

"I will, *patron*." he said, and quickly ran toward Paradise.

"What are we going to do?" Martin asked, riding up alongside Slocum.

"Go back up the road to the spring tank, water our stock, and stay out of sight." Had he done the right thing sending the boy? He certainly hoped so. Rafael was very clever and experienced beyond his years. Slocum probably owed his life to the boy for his quick intervention with Curly Bill and Ringo. Slocum looked again at the tops of the wood-front facades. He hoped he'd done the right thing.

After sunset, Slocum sat on a large rock with a good view of the road, drawing on his cigar, the red glow visible in the darkness. Someone was coming. He hoped it was the boy. He shifted so he could draw his gun if it proved to be someone else.

"*Patron?*" a small voice whispered in the darkness.

"Over here, Rafael."

"Where is Señor Martin?" The youth looked around for the man.

"Taking a nap. I was watching for you. What did you learn?"

"Those men, Lee and Pepper Bill, are staying in a small *casa* up the canyon."

"Is she there?" he asked, his heart pounding in his chest.

"One sits on the porch with shotgun. I was afraid to get closer, but why would they guard such a poor place?"

"You did good. Let's wake up Martin." He felt better about the situation as they hurried up the draw. There was no reason to guard a shack in this country unless you had a prize inside. *We're coming, Lucia.* "How far is it?"

"Across the ridge and around up this canyon." The boy pointed to the north.

"Can we lead our horses close?"

"*Sí.*"

"Get up, Martin." Slocum dropped to his knee to awaken the man on the bedroll. "He's found where they have her."

"I knew he would." Martin rose to his knees and began to roll up the blankets. "We going to get her?"

"Yes, we'll lead the horses close. Then we'll have to figure out how to draw the guard off."

"Good."

"I have an idea," Rafael said, undoing the leads of their horses. "Why not send that big mule up to the porch and let him get a hold of him."

"Can we do that?" Slocum asked.

"Sure, he'll go to their horses," Martin said, undoing the mule's lead, which Rafael had not bothered with. Respect for the big animal's fearsome actions had kept the boy out of the red mule's range.

"Lead the way," Slocum said to the youth. With Curly Bill's dun's reins in one hand and his bay's lead rope in the other, Slocum fell in behind the gray and Ringo's black, which Rafael led. Martin brought up the rear with his big mule.

Out of nowhere, the mule began to hee-haw so loud it hurt Slocum's ears. He grinned as he followed the boy up the mountainside; it was playing right into his plans. The guard could expect a large mule coming to visit him, since he had heard the raucous call several times before the animal even showed up.

Finally, their horses hitched in the junipers, they led the mule to the draw that led to the cabin.

"You give the boy and me time to get up there. Then you send old Red up there to visit with that shotgun guard," Slocum told Martin.

"What if it don't work?"

"Then we'll think of a new way to take them. I believe it will work."

"I'll do it."

"Good, come on, Rafael. Keep your head down. A scattergun does bad things to one's body."

Slocum didn't wait for his reply. He hurried up through the towering junipers. To catch their breath, they rested where he could see the shape of the shack from the security of the boughs.

The front porch was dark, and he couldn't make out anyone seated on it. Then, as if pulled by some unseen strings, a shadowy someone walked to the edge and spat tobacco. Starlight glinted on the gun barrel in the man's arms.

Wordlessly, Slocum shared a nod with Rafael. Then he pushed the boy back in the branches out of harm's way as the braying mule came up the draw.

"What the hell's coming?" someone asked as the door creaked open. It was still too dark for Slocum to see a thing.

"A damn big mule. He's been honking out there for an hour," a younger voice said, obviously the one with the shotgun.

"He got a damn rider?"

"Naw, just a loose mule. See him, he's big as an elephant."

"Sum-bitch, he's worth some bucks. Go catch him."

"Here, hold the scattergun," the kid said, and jumped off the porch to catch Red.

Not prepared for the greeting, Red whirled and drove the kid through the air with both hind feet. He landed on his butt short of the porch, and Pepper Bill hurried off to see about his partner. Slocum cut down on them, and his shot in the dust took both men by surprise. Bill threw the shotgun away in his haste to raise his hands, and the stunned Tyler Lee hugged his gut, swearing about the whole thing being a trick, a damn trick.

"I got them covered," Martin shouted, which sent Slocum rushing inside the dark shack.

"Lucia?' he whispered in the darkness. A knot formed in his stomach. What if she wasn't here? He closed his eyes. Where was she?

"Slocum, come untie me."

He struck a lucifer on the table, then torched a candle as he saw her tear-streaked face in the flickering light. Seated in a straight-back chair with her arms bound, she looked as regal as she had dismounting the stage in Tombstone.

"You need your knife, señor?" Rafael asked, joining them.

"Cut her loose, partner," Slocum said, kneeling before her. "I swear, Lucia, I've been coming for days."

"I knew you were," she said as they pulled away the ropes that the boy cut behind her back.

"Doc had gotten the ransom money. What were they waiting on?"

"They didn't want to share any of it with Ike. They were more worried *he'd* come find me than *you*."

"There's not a helluva lot of honor among thieves?"

"No, there isn't. Who is this young man."

"Your new *segundo*, Rafael."

The boy made a gracious bow at the waist, then straightened and beamed. "My sister Maria is at the ranch. She is much worried about you."

"I can't wait to meet her," she said, and tousled his hair.

"This is Billy Ray Martin, the man freighting the lumber from the mill."

"I guess I owe all of you a lot," she said.

"No, ma'am, you don't owe us a thing. Why, we've had a passel of fun treeing these cowboys coming here." Martin removed his felt hat and motioned to Slocum.

"We going to hang them two like we did the others?"

"Hang them?" Her face paled in the candlelight.

"I meant by their heels," Martin explained. "Like we did Curly Bill and Ringo. It don't kill them if someone finds them in time."

"Kidnapping is a serious offense. We get them back to Tombstone, we should be able to press charges." Slocum considered the future for the pair. "Some time in Yuma might do both of them good."

"Have you eaten?" she asked, standing close to him.

"No."

"Then I'll cook something. We can't do anything until daylight now, can we?" she asked.

"No, that'll be soon enough. Martin, you take first watch. Rafael, get all our horses down here. Those two tied up good?"

"They ain't going anywhere," Martin promised, and headed out the door after the youth.

When they were alone at last, her arms encircled his neck and her honey lips meet his. He closed his eyes and savored the sweetness. At last she was safe. Her shapely form tight against him, he felt the tension of the past days drain from him.

24

They arrived at Lucia's ranch the next evening. Pepper Bill and Tyler Lee, tied together, rode double on Ringo's horse. The prisoners' obvious sour looks almost made Slocum laugh out loud. Jose came out with a rifle and then, seeing his *patron* in the lead, shouted for the others.

Maria ran out so fast she beat the others handily, and soon walked beside Slocum's stirrups.

"You found her safe?" Maria used the side of her hand to shade her eyes against the late sun as she looked up at him.

"There she is. Lucia, this is the sweet girl Maria. Rafael's sister."

"So nice to meet you, Maria. Slocum has spoken so well of you. I'm sorry for all the trouble. But we will get to be good friends soon, I hope."

"Gracias, señora," she said, and then bowed her head as she walked between them. She kept her dark eyes

averted from her new boss as she held onto Slocum's boot.

"I understand you are disappointed with this ranch," Lucia said. "But I know we can make it a good one."

"Oh, yes, señora."

"We will have a good ranch here," Lucia assured her, and then stepped down from her horse, giving the reins to Slocum. Hand in hand with Maria on one side, and with one of Jose's children's holding her fingers on the other side, she headed for the current ranch headquarters—the one-room shack.

"There is much to do here," Maria said.

Lucia looked back over her shoulder and grinned privately at Slocum. He saw the pride and pleasure that she had found almost instantly with her new family. "Yes, Maria, lots for all of us to do to make this a great ranch." Then she was moving off, with Maria and the children around her skirt as she talked to them like a schoolteacher.

"Grande hacienda," Maria said, and Lucia nodded as the children began asking questions.

Slocum stepped off the dun, undid the girth, and dumped the saddle on its horn. Then he piled the sweat-soaked blankets on top to dry. He was pleased with Lucia's acceptance of her ranch help, and was busy musing to himself about what to do next when Martin cleared his throat.

"We taking them two to the sheriff tomorrow?" Martin asked.

"I can do that. You still have lots of lumber to haul."

"Damn, Slocum, it's going to be hard to go back to driving mules after all this excitement."

"It's a lot safer. Besides, China Annie has some carpenters ready to drive nails, when you get all the material up here."

"Guess you're right. Climb down, you two. We have your accommodations right over here," Martin said to the two outlaws. He ushered them to a large juniper tree to tie them to its base for the night.

In the morning, Slocum would surrender them to Behan's jurisdiction for better or worse. The fact that they'd planned to double-cross Ike Clanton might make it worse. When that became known, they wouldn't live long in Cochise County, and Yuma Prison might even be a relief.

That evening, Slocum walked Lucia to the rise above the ranch. They found a large flat boulder to sit on, letting their legs hang over the edge. The cool night wind lifted her long dark hair, and she combed away strands of it with her fingers to clear her face.

"Landon is dead," she finally said. "I learned that from the prisoners."

"Lead poisoning?"

"Yes. A shotgun blast from a stage guard, they said. He died in the arms of a harlot named Sarah."

"I guess you'll never know what made him do what he did."

She shook her head, and in the starlight. He noticed her chin tremble.

"Do you want to return to Chicago?" he asked.

"No, these people will be my family. I want a real ranch here. I have my inheritance."

"I'm taking those two to Tombstone tomorrow. You may have to testify in case of a trial." He wanted her to know the possible repercussions of his actions.

"I'll be ready for that too."

"I've told you before, I can't stay here. I may have stayed here too long as it is."

She nodded that she understood, but turned away from him.

"It's not how I want it," he said, not finding the words he wished for.

"I understand," she managed.

"I have the lumber coming."

She twisted around and then threw her arms around his neck. "Quit talking."

"Yes, ma'am." And they sprawled on top of the great rock in each other's embrace.

• • •

Tombstone basked in the heat of summer. Dust from the ore wagons rose like smoke from a grass fire as the traffic either headed to the crusher or hurried away for more ore. Slocum dismounted at the courthouse and pushed the two prisoners inside. He checked around for any familiar faces, then drove the pair to Behan's office.

"Let me get this right. You are charging these two citizens with kidnapping?" the deputy asked from behind the desk as if the entire matter was somehow unbelievable.

"Yes, he is, and I'm ready to prosecute," Virgil Earp said in the open doorway with a grim voice. "I saw you come up Fremont with them two, Slocum, and hurried over. How is she?"

"Mrs. McClain is fine."

"Good. Did these two say anything?"

"They planned to double-cross Ike," Slocum said under his breath. "And keep the money for themselves."

"Oh, really?" Virgil twisted the end of his mustache, and a small smile formed in the corner of his mouth. "By the way, Curly Bill Brocious and Johnny Ringo showed up a day ago, claimed you'd robbed them and stole their horses, then left them hanging by their heels. They come in on the mail buckboard."

"I guess the table was turned."

"Sure was. Mail rider said he cut them down. Doc and I figured you'd be coming along." The twinkle in his blue eyes danced with mischief and amusement.

"They make any charges here against me?"

"Hell, no. Just talk."

"I've got to make out all these damn papers," the deputy complained, holding his hands up like he was lost.

"Lock the sum-bitches up. I'll be back and fill out the damn papers. And Deputy?" Virgil looked the man hard in the eye.

"Yes?"

"You be damn sure that they don't drift out that back door. Hear me?" Earp said it sharp enough and loud enough that the desk man nodded and swallowed at the same time. "Come on, we need to find Doc," Virgil said to Slocum. "He's got something to talk to you about."

Slocum rode the dun up Allen Street wondering if Curly Bill was anywhere about. He led the extra horses he'd brought in the prisoners on. He hitched them in front of the Oriental, and waited for the long-striding Virgil to catch up with him.

They entered the bat-wing doors, and Doc strode over pompously with a bottle and glasses.

"Gentleman, let us drink to the glory days!"

"What glory days?" Slocum asked.

"Sah, we may be on the very brink of ridding this land of the insidious pests that are robbing and stealing from everyone."

"The Clantons?"

"Them and the Lowerys as well," Doc declared.

"I'll drink to that."

"The lady is no doubt in good health?" Doc inquired, pouring liquor in Slocum's glass.

"Considering all she's been through, she's in very good spirits. Now what is the plan?"

"All in good time, sah."

"He brought in Pepper Bill and that Tyler Lee for the kidnapping," Virgil added, taking two finger in his glass and then downing it. "Behan's deputy down there wanted to release them."

"Shame, we can't cure all of it. This calls for a few friendly drinks first."

Slocum savored the whiskey. Better than most. He had plenty of time. Whatever Doc had in mind for the Cowboys suited him. Nothing short of death would stop them. He let the firewater slip down his throat, warm his ears, and settle his nerves. Yes, it would be interesting, whatever Holliday had in mind to resolve the matter.

25

"Señor Carillo, this is the man we mentioned," Doc said as three men sat on their horses on the point off the Bisbee Road. It was early morning and no one was in sight. They remained mounted for the meeting.

The man under the flat-brim hat had the eyes of an eagle as he nodded coldly. His big dappled-gray horse shifted anxiously under his leather clad legs; the roller bit clacked on the horse's molars as he bobbed his head, ready to be on the way.

"He's tangled with Ike and won before," Doc said, indicating Slocum.

"Good. But the less people who know our business the better," Carillo said. The coldness of the man's manner convinced Slocum he had a purpose that was not to be dissuaded by heaven or earth. Anyone or anything that stood in his way he would flatten.

"Slocum can be trusted," Doc said. His bay laid back his ears and threatened the gray, but a slap from Doc with the reins straightened the animal for the moment.

"When the next dark of the moon comes, we will meet in Arido. No one is to know the day or the time. Have your people ready to ride. Just so they Clantons aren't warned. I plan for all the Clantons to be there."

"Need any help from us on that?" Doc asked.

"No. You bring the men and guns when the time is at hand. Remember. No one, I mean no one, is to know when we plan to strike or our plan will fail."

Under the man's hard gaze, Slocum nodded that he understood.

"I have seen you before?" Carillo asked, looking hard at him.

"Perhaps," Slocum said to dismiss the man's interest. He too recalled their past meeting while in the Sierra Madras chasing Geronimo with Lt. Gatewood.

"You were a scout for the U.S. Army," Carillo said.

"Right, and you were looking for a boy they took."

Carillo nodded and said no more. Obviously the man's search for his son had ended without success. Apaches seldom kept young captives unless they were very tough and matched their own endurance.

"We will have six good men," Doc said, and then he began to cough into a kerchief. The spell passed and he straightened in the saddle, checking his pawing bay. "They will be armed and ready."

"To better days, amigos," Carillo said. Then, as if satisfied, he touched his hat, turned his gray, and was gone.

Slocum watched him move across the brown grassland with the smoothness of something mechanical. Swift and powerful, the rider and horse soon were gone to the south in the glare of the morning sun.

"I guess you figured out enough by now. He wants Finn and Ike, the damn Lowerys, Curly Bill and his bunch all gathered at Old Man Clanton's in Mexico, then we sweep in and end them once and for all."

"All planned out, huh?"

"You don't have to go."

"I will."

"I figured we could count you in. It should end the Clantons' reign of terror. Let's ride. I need to tell the sixth man."

"Fine, I guess it's the only way to ever stop them."

"The only way. You know John Slaughter?" Doc asked.

"No."

"Then you'll meet him."

"He's in the deal too?"

"Yes." Doc set off to the west. Slocum took a last look in the direction of Mexico and imagined he glimpsed the rider and gray top a rise and then disappear in the sea that stretched to the towering Huachucha Mountains. He set Curly Bill's dun after Doc in a short lope.

Slaughter's Ranch was on Patagonia Creek. In late afternoon, they reached the adobe structures and pole corrals. A lovely young woman came out onto the porch and welcomed them.

"Nice to see you, Doc," she said, and then she smiled at Slocum.

"Mrs. Slaughter. Meet my good friend Slocum." Doc quickly dismounted and removed his hat.

"My pleasure, sir," she said, extending her long fingers in a firm grasp as Slocum held his hat and reins in the other hand. "John should be back soon. He rode up to check on some new bulls. Come on the porch, I have some sweet, cool lemon water. It would be good for your cough too," she said like a mother to Doc, who had tried to privately show his disdain for the drink. "This world would be a better place sipping lemon water than spirits."

"Ma'am, I am certain that it would be." Doc made a big sweeping bow to her.

"Don't you act condescending to me, Doc Holliday," she scolded him, pouring a large fancy crystal glass full of the yellow drink. She handed it to Slocum, who had seen a small man ride up on a lanky horse.

In his late forties, John Slaughter was a wiry man, about five-foot-six, behind a walrus mustache and a high crown hat. He dismounted, hitched his horse and came up on the veranda. His obvious shortness disappeared when he smiled and acknowledged Doc, shaking his hand, then Slocum's.

He took a glass of lemonade from her with some disdain, but as if to save an argument in front of company, he didn't say a thing about it. Slaughter motioned them to the chairs on the porch, hung his hat on the corner post of one and assumed a seat.

"Thanks, my dear," he said hoisting the glass up for her to see as she stood in the doorway.,

"Gentlemen, supper shall be ready in a half hour, so talk fast." She smiled angelically and went inside.

"Yes, my dear," Slaughter said. Then he turned to Doc and spoke in a low voice as the three men sat on the edge of their chairs. "Well, have we set a time?"

"Dark of the moon," Doc said.

"Good," Slaughter said, looking up and searching both of their faces. "We have to end this once and for all. Carillo wants them out of Mexico. We don't need them raiding and running roughshod over everyone in this country either."

"There's Virgil, Wyatt and Morgan, Earp and Slocum and you and I."

"My man Bat will be there. He's good as any white man," Slaughter said. Then he sipped on the lemonade, made a face of displeasure, and after that forced a grin. "This tastes close to medicine to me. We'll be ready then with our part."

"That makes seven of us." Doc set his lemonade down on the small table. Obviously he had no intention of drinking any of it. Slocum's lemonade slipped coolly past his tongue, and he rather enjoyed the sour-sweetness.

"That's enough guns?" Slaughter asked.

"I'm certain it is. Carillo is concerned that someone will warn them. He plans to trick Finn and Ike to go up there. He'd like Ringo and Brocious there too."

"He wants Christmas," Slaughter said, shaking his

head as if that would be impossible. "I won't even tell my man until we are ready to go."

"The Earps won't say a thing."

"Guess that leaves Doc and me," Slocum said softly. He set the empty glass down on the table.

"I've heard about you, Slocum. Hung Curly Bill and Ringo by their heels for half a day. Sent Ike into the prickly pear. It's a wonder you still are alive." The man gave him a genuine smile.

"It didn't do any good."

"How do you know? You threw them off balance. They were running roughshod over the entire county. They have pulled in their horns some."

"But not completely," Doc said pointedly.

"Yes, not completely," Slaughter agreed.

"Supper, gentlemen," Slaughter's wife called from the door.

"We're coming, my dear," Slaughter said as they rose to their feet. Then, under his breath, he added, "To peace in Cochise County."

"Yes."

Slocum let them go first. He looked off toward the Whetstones beyond the rustling cottonwoods. This was to be the final chapter for the Cowboys. He would be there. A moment of envy for the short Texan's lot tore at him. He thought about Slaughter's lovely ranch and wife. If he could only do the same thing with Lucia McClain.

"You are the wind." The Apache's words echoed in his ears as the evening breeze swept his face.

"Mr. Slocum, may I take your hat?" she asked.

"Oh, yes, ma'am," he said, snatching it off. A quick sickness soured his stomach as he gazed at her beauty and watched her stand on her toes to hang the hat on the mule-deer antlers in the hall. Why couldn't he simply stay in this land of sun and hot winds? Have a bed of his own? A woman like her to hostess his guests?

"Come, supper will get cold," she said, and with a swish of her gray skirt led him to the dining room.

Then he saw the lace curtains being held out by the

wind, and he knew this would never be his lot. No fancy long table of oak, set with an embroidered tablecloth, fancy china plates, and real silverware beside each place. The rich aroma of her beef roast cleared his nose of the desert dust, and he recalled the same smells in his mother's dining room.

He remembered Alabama, and his childhood days growing up. Was he there again? Black servants hustling about to put food on the table. His father upset that he had slipped away from his studies to catch catfish in the bayou, dissect a bird for the secret of his flight, or climb the tallest oak on the plantation to try to see Tennessee.

Then the cannons roared, the cannons of war, and the curtain closed on the boy's past. He was filling his plate beside Doc and looking at the sweet smile of Mrs. Slaughter. Two children in their teens had joined them for supper. Will, the boy, was a lanky freckled version of his father. The girl was a proper young lady. These were not the children of the young wife, but nonetheless they were very well mannered toward her, and acted affectionate too.

Slocum savored the rich food as Doc inquired about the two children's teeth. They told him that they had no pain, and from then on barely opened their mouths, obviously from fear that Doc might see something wrong and want to examine them.

After supper the children and the wife excused themselves, and the men drank whiskey in short tumblers on the veranda in the coolness sweeping down the valley. It was good rye, and as smooth as any Slocum could recall having in years. Obviously Slaughter had his sources. He and Slaughter smoked good cigars as well.

"Spend the night, men?" Slaughter offered, but Doc denied the request.

"Less we see of each other together, the better we shall be," Holliday said.

"Indeed," Slaughter agreed, and then he shook hands with Slocum. "Nice to have you and the others on my side."

"It's good to be there and to meet you. Thank your wife. It was a fine meal." Slocum reset his hat and started off the porch.

"Anytime you're in the area, come by. We may sell this place soon."

"Oh?"

"In six months you should find me over on the San Bernadino. I am in the process of buying that land grant from the Perez family."

"More reason to be rid of the Clantons," Doc said, fixing his cinch.

"Yes, they've used that land as a corridor with an open door to drive stolen cattle up from Mexico. But come by when you're in the country," Slaughter said.

"I shall. Good luck with your new ranch."

"I shall need it. The renegades use that valley too."

Slocum nodded. He did not need to tell the man about the Apaches. They used that way frequently escaping to Mexico. No doubt they had kept the Perez family from ever living for very long on their land grant. He had even bathed in the big springs near the ruins of the hacienda the Apaches had burned to the ground. Slaughter no doubt had a good plan for using and holding it. Slocum felt certain about that after spending the past few hours with the man.

"Tough, ain't he?" Doc said as they headed for the far-off pass between the Whetstones and the Mustang Mountains in the pearly starlight.

"If I was going to have a man at my gun hand, he'd sure fit the bill."

"He will do, sah. He damn sure will do."

26

There were six Chinese workers, who never stopped talking in their native tongue, and a wagon load of supplies. Slocum had hired a teamster by the name of Dunagan to freight it all up to Lucia's ranch. The Ap was in the shafts of the small buckboard he'd bought for her to use. No one was about to buy the crazy spoiled horse anyway, so she might as well have him to drive. With the dun and a bay saddlehorse hitched behind for his use later, he had left in the buckboard from Tombstone before daylight. The slick taste of road dust was on his tongue when, in late afternoon, he was relieved to finally enter the canyon that led up into the mountains to her ranch.

He slapped the Ap on the rump to set him into a trot. They'd be there for supper and that suited him. If he outdistanced the teamster and the Chinese, so much the better. He was concerned how long he could listen to that talk of theirs, which he couldn't understand, going on at about a hundred miles an hour.

There was no word on Ike Clanton. No one in Tombstone had seen or heard of him in weeks. Obviously he was still healing, or still plucking needles out of himself. Drunk, Billy Clanton had been bragging in the bars that the Earps would soon be taken care of. Just Billy's wishful thinking, according to Virgil.

Seeing riders ahead, Slocum went for his Colt. The hard rubber handle filled his fist. Then he saw it was Ike and another man. They both raised their hands at the sight of his swift draw. What were they doing up there? Was Lucia safe? A moment of rage at the notion that Ike might try something against her made his shoulders shake with rage.

"We meet again, big man," Ike said. No mistaking the hatred glinting in his pig eyes.

Slocum never answered him. He held the reins in one hand, the Colt in the other. The other man was Tom Lowery. He'd been pointed out to Slocum before by Virgil or Doc.

'We're just minding our business," Ike said. "I'm damn near willing to forgive you."

"Listen, you backshooter. I catch you up here in these mountains again, you better have your undertaker fees paid."

"It's a free country. You don't own them."

"You aren't listening, Ike. I said I ever saw your butt in these mountains anywhere ever again, there would be a maker in the cemetery for you."

"You—you—I should have shot your ass in Gleason."

"Come on, Ike. He's mad is all." Lowery rode in between the two and guided Ike to the side of the tracks.

"Mad isn't the word." Slocum rose to his feet in the wagon. "Any man sends a backshooter after me better be ready for something worse."

"I never—"

"Come on, Ike," Lowery said, acting anxious to avoid a fight as he herded him around Slocum's rig.

A damn good thing, Slocum thought. He twisted in the seat to watch them ride off toward the base of the moun-

tains. When they were out of sight, he holstered his handgun and clucked to the Ap.

What were they doing up there? That was something
he intended to find out before he met Doc and the others
for the big ride south. He had five days left before the
dark of the moon. Ike had something going on in those
mountains, and it could only be bad.

The children rushed in excitement to greet him. Lucia
came to the door of her tent. He had found her an army
officer's shelter, and she used it for her residence. Smiling, skirt in hand, she hurried to greet him. Combing back
her long hair through her fingers, she acted almost uncomfortable in his presence when he turned from hitching
the Ap to the post.

"Something wrong?" he asked quietly over the shouts
and cheers of the children about them.

"No," she said with a pouting lower lip.

"Has Ike been here?"

"No, why?" She blinked at him in disbelief.

"I met him on the canyon road."

"Like before?" She frowned, looking concerned.

"Close to there. Is everyone here all right?"

"Yes, fine."

"Good," he said, hugging her lightly by the waist.

Her arms flew around his neck. "You were gone for
so long."

"I warned you—"

Her lips sealed off his words. The tip of her tongue
sought his mouth, and he closed his eyes to the brilliant
sun filtering through the live oaks. Damn, oh, damn, why
couldn't he stay?

A few hours later, his crew arrived. With no time to
spare, the main house was marked out on the ground.
Sooie, the head of the six-man crew, agreed with Lucia's
pencil sketches. He could build one like that. Yes, the
lumber was good. But he needed this and that. Slocum
waved his concerns away.

"I want to backtrack Ike," he said about mid-afternoon

when he and Lucia were alone seated on their rock. "Something is going on and I want to know why he rides out of these mountains."

"When will you be back?" she asked.

"As soon as I can be."

"You better come to my tent when you do," she warned.

"I will."

"Good." She winked mischievously at him. They went to the corral together and he saddled the bay. He wanted to save the dun for the hard ride ahead.

"Be careful," she said, and pounded his upper leg with her fist to make her point before he swung the horse away to leave. He looked at her as she idly reset her hair with her fingers.

"I will be back."

She gave him a warning look, and then he rode away. He'd learned Jose and Rafael were up on the mountain unplugging a spring. Maria had gone along to look for some berries to make jam with.

He rode down to the wagon tracks, and soon he could no longer hear the Chinese chatter, nor the shouts of Jose's children. Only the song of the wren and occasional dove or quail that rode the warm wind of the afternoon.

Ike's hoofprints came from the east. The wagon tracks that sliced the dried grass ended at an old mine claim up a large side canyon several miles south of the ranch. Slocum was forced to dismount and search for where the back trail came from among the pilings and weathered wooden shacks.

Why did Ike always ride west out of the Swisshelms? All the prints, even the old ones, were headed toward Tombstone. Why did Ike always ride down the canyon and never up it?

He removed his hat, scratched the top of his head, and looked around at the empty ramshackle buildings. This wasn't what brought Ike up there. Slocum searched the timbered slopes for a sign of a trail. Most of the big trees had been cut for the mine's usage.

Then behind what must have once been the cookshack, he found a well-used single trail going up the mountain's face. With no one in sight, he mounted the bay and set out up the slope following the beaten pathway. It still made no sense, but Ike had a reason for coming over this way.

In an hour, Slocum was high in the pass. A cool wind swept his face as he looked across the San Bernadino Valley toward New Mexico. He'd jumped a mule deer and her fawn while coming up—they'd fled into the trees. He'd let the gelding have his head going upgrade, and he let him blow on top.

Leaning back in the saddle, Slocum started down the steep mountainside. He was careful to stop and examine what was ahead and below so he didn't ride into a trap, and in a short while he could hear cattle bawling further down the mountain. Dust boiled up from far below.

Stolen cattle—had to be the reason. Slocum felt confident as he dropped off the mountain that he had found Ike's main camp. He tied the bay in the timber, and crawled out on a large flat rock to study the canyon below.

Four or five punchers were roping and branding, using a wet gunnysack to alter brands, as he could see through a brass telescope. No one looked on guard, and they acted very busy with their jobs. If they were occupied and had no lookouts, he might manage to slip in and cause some trouble. No one was close enough to help him—it was up to him.

He remounted the bay to move in closer. When he was satisfied he had to go the rest of the way on foot, he secured the horse in a side canyon and then began to slip up Indian-fashion on the rustlers.

He found the cook busy making bread in camp.

"Grab some sky, hombre!" he ordered.

In a shower of flour, the man raised his hands, nearly dancing on his toes. "What you want anyway?" The man's high-pitched voice rang almost soprano.

"I come to hang some rustlers."

"Oh, sweet Jesus, not me." The man began to tremble. "I'm just the cook, sir."

"If you could ride to Silver City fast enough, you'd be out of my jurisdiction," Slocum said, acting the role of lawman for the man's benefit.

"Hell, I could get there fast."

"How fast?"

"So damn fast it would blur your eyes."

"You give one word of warning to those boys, you're a dead cook, savvy?"

"I'll be gone so damn fast you'll think I'm a dust devil."

"You got two minutes to saddle and ride."

"From now?"

"Go!"

"Yes, sir. I'm only the damn cook. I ain't never stole no cows." The man went off muttering to himself.

He threw an old hull of a saddle on a horse in the pen, and shakily he mounted up and rode out down the canyon at a long trot. Slocum was satisfied from the way the man beat the horse that he was not going to stop until he got to New Mexico.

The cook was gone. Next the rustlers. Slocum helped himself to some raisin-bread pudding on the board. He ate the bowl slowly. When those boys came in for supper he had a plan—it wouldn't involve food either.

"Charlie? Where the hell are you at?" someone called.

"Ease over here and don't try nothing," Slocum ordered with his gun hand full.

"Who the hell are you?"

"The man who's going to blow your butt away if you don't listen. Get over here." Impatient, Slocum waved him over with his pistol.

"Where's Charlie?" the young man asked in a daze.

"He's gone to Silver City," Slocum said, disarming him.

"Why the hell he go there?"

"To keep from being lynched for rustling."

"You the law?"

"What do I look like?"

"The law."

"Sit down on the ground. Don't move a muscle. If you warn the others you are dead, savvy?"

"Yes."

"Hey, where's that damn lazy Charlie?" the next rider asked, dismounting and busy shucking his gloves. "You deaf, Pete? I asked—"

"Hands up and step over here."

"Sum-bitch, who are you?" the puncher asked, taken aback as Slocum spun him around, took his gun and knife, and then pushed him to sit beside the other one.

"Not one word or you're dead."

"Where did he come from?" the second one hissed to Pete.

"Shut up."

Silence reigned.

The other three dismounted and were busy talking when Slocum stepped out from behind the chuck wagon.

"Hands in the sky or get ready to meet your maker."

"Who in the hell?" They blinked in disbelief.

He punctuated his threat with a bullet at their feet that made their mounts shy backwards and clear the field. Relieved at his success, he felt more in charge as they paraded over and he removed their artillery.

"What the hell do you want, mister?" the oldest rustler demanded.

"We're closing you up in Arizona. Ike ain't going to be able to pay you since he'll be in jail shortly. You boys can expect a few years roasting in Yuma for your hard work. I hear they can fry eggs in there and never light a stove."

"Where's Charlie? Did you kill him?"

"No." Slocum shook his head. "Charlie had a health problem. A constriction of the throat. He thought that Silver City might be healthier climate than here."

"We got the same choice?"

"If you're smart enough not to look back and keep on riding."

"Hey, mister, we're that smart."

"One at a time. You." He motioned to Pete. "Get on your horse and show them the way to New Mexico."

"No shooting me in the back?" the wide-eyed youth asked.

"Can you ride like hell?" Slocum asked him.

"Damn right." The youth jumped up, hat in hand, and ran to his horse. On the second try, he mounted it and screaming like a banshee, raced down the canyon beating his pony on the butt with his hat.

"You're next," Slocum said to the second oldest-looking hand.

"Yes, sir!" He stumbled, half fell, but in his wild lunges managed to recover and capture his wide-eyed pony by the reins.

"Listen, any of you come back, you'll hang. Am I understood?" he asked the remaining outlaws.

"Yes," came the chorus as pandemonium broke out in their efforts to flee. Two of the rustlers' horses went to bucking in their flight.

"I'm leaving, dammit. I'm leaving!" one of the riders on a bucker shouted back at Slocum.

Slocum finished his second bowl of raisin-bread pudding. Not bad. Charlie wasn't such a sorry cook. He'd had worse. Then he rode up and set the remuda loose, by cutting the rope strung through the iron stakes. He loose-herded the horses toward the valley. Next, he let down the bars on the fence that held the herd of stolen cattle in the canyon.

With an eye out for any trouble, he sent the cattle and calves eastward through the gap. It would take Ike a week and plenty of hands to ever gather them again. Slocum rode along in the long shadows. The sunset was sparkling over the peaks when he set the gelding headed back over the mountains.

He would wake Lucia in the tent. He slumped in the saddle. *I'm coming, Lucia. After midnight or so, darling.*

27

He had prepared the dun for the long ride. The shoes had been reset on all four feet. He had expected Ike to do something angry over the loss of his herd. But there'd been no sign of the man. Maybe he didn't realize they were gone yet. Or better, Carillo had lured all of them to join the old man in Mexico. Anxious to learn more, Slocum strapped on his bedroll.

"You won't be gone long?" she asked above the hammering and sawing sounds nearby. The fresh wood framework of her new home was fast taking shape. Martin had brought more wood in the day before, and left with Sooie's order for more that morning. The freighter had seen nothing of Ike or Curly Bill, and was uneasy, wondering what they were up to.

"I warned you," Slocum said.

"But you came back each time." She moved in, adjusted his vest, and then swept his hat off his head. Holding it behind her, she stood on her toes for him to kiss her good-bye.

"It might not work this time," he said.

"But why?"

"There are things that happened a long time ago that can never be straightened out."

"There's lawyers, there are judges, I have money."

He took his hat from her and brushed some of the dust off the brim. Nothing he could say or do would change the facts. A final soft kiss on the side of her face, and then he mounted up. The knot in his throat would not go away.

"It will be a nice house," he said, admiring it before riding out.

"There is room for you."

"Good."

"You will be back?"

"I can't promise that."

"God be with you," she said. Then, about to cry and chewing on her lip, she ran for the tent.

Maria waved from the new framework to him. Rafael and Jose were gone for firewood. The ranch had begun to take shape. She would someday have a great hacienda. *Grande.*

Tombstone sounded the same as he rode up Fremont and turned on Fourth. The tinny pianos, banjos, and fiddles creaked through the night. Raucous-voiced whores screamed like hellcats set loose, and some Irish baritone sang "Greensleeves," making a dozen drunk miners cry in their beer at his ability.

Past the hanging tree in front of the *Epitaph* office, he saw in the glimmer of light the blanket butt of a big Ap horse hitched on the Palace side of the street. There was a white-and-black leopard marking he knew anywhere. Lyle and Ferrel Abbott were in town.

The damn Ft. Scott, Kansas, bounty hunters were there. How much did they know about his business? He needed to get word inside to Doc. Would it be safe for him to slip into the Oriental Saloon? Cautiously, he dismounted in the shadows between the two saloons, not anxious to draw any light or attention on himself.

From his saddlebag, he drew out a piece of brown paper. He took the stub of a lead pencil from the saddlebag, licked twice to get it started, then wrote a cryptic note:

Doc
Come to Pasco's. I got a problem.

He signed it with an S.

He waited until one of the saloon girls came down the sidewalk headed for work.

"Hey, honey," he said softly.

She paused, considered him, and then moved in for business. Her exploring hand cupped and felt the bulge in his pants as she nibbled on his neck. A heavy dose of lavender perfume cut his breathing.

"You ain't half bad, cowboy."

"For ten bucks, can you keep your mouth shut?" he asked, holding her close like a man about to work himself up to going to her crib.

"For ten bucks I'd drop your pants right here and play a tune on it, honey."

"Wish I had time to do that, but I don't. Take this note to Doc Holliday. Ten bucks is yours."

"Why, I'd like to earn it," she said, wiggling her shoulder to make her breasts shake and then rubbing his fly with more effort.

"You listening?" he asked.

"Damn right. This note goes to Holliday, but when do I get you?"

"I'll be around for mine."

"Ask for Sharon, Rose of Sharon. You won't ever regret it."

He clapped her on the butt as she started to leave. She

grinned big, then sashayed off down the dark boardwalk. He undid the horse after checking the street and far porch of the Palace for any sign of the Abbotts. Slowly he started walking back to Pasco's a block away.

28

"What the hell is wrong, sah?" Doc asked as he came into the dark shed.

"Two bounty hunters just arrived in town. They have their damn horses hitched on the Palace side of Fourth Street."

"Damn, you have whipped Curly Bill Brocious. Hung that blubber-gut up by his heels. Did the same to Johnny Ringo, the absolute terror of Ft. Griffin, Texas. I mean, Ringo treed that damn hellhole. You forced that cowardly Ike Clanton to dive into a cactus patch, and what else. Two damn bounty hunters have you standing in the dark. My Gawd, they must be tougher than nails."

Slocum shook his head. "I'll not kill them unless there isn't any other way. I've avoided them for years."

"Sah, here, have glass of good whiskey." Doc held the glass and bottle out the open doorway so he see clearly enough to pour. Then he gave him the tumbler of whiskey. "I shall send the two on a wild-goose chase. Later tonight, we're all riding to a camp Slaughter has on his new holdings."

"Good, send them two to Nogales."

"A good destination for them. Opposite, of course, from ours. Their names?"

"Abbott. Ferrel is the younger one, Lyle the big-gutted one."

"Yes, Lyle and Ferrel Abbott. They are headed for the Santa Cruz River Valley." Doc did a few fancy dance steps on the hay underfoot, waving the bottle like it was his partner. "Taken care of, my good man."

Slocum only wished it was that easy. Still, Doc could perform feats few men could accomplish. He smiled and toasted him.

"I'll meet you all on the road to Bisbee," Slocum said.

"Rumors reached us today. A band of ranchers raided Ike's cow camp in Texas Canyon. You hear anything."

"Sent his cowboys packing to New Mexico?"

"Yes, exactly, sir."

"Scattered his remuda and the stolen cattle?"

"Sounds similar. Why, sah, it must have taken twenty angry men to storm that cow camp?"

"They mention the raisin-bread pudding they helped themselves to?"

"No."

"They ate it too."

"Obviously then, you heard about it. Ike was as drunk as a hooter tonight, ready to burn them all out if he can learn their identity." Doc refilled his glass.

"He never let that stop him before."

"Watch for us on the Bisbee Road in a few hours. I'll see to the Abbotts."

"Thanks, Doc," he said, and then he downed the whiskey. They'd be handled, but when this Mexican affair was over, he needed to hit the trail. *Damn, Lucia, I warned you. Our time's up.*

29

Clouds shrouded the starlight. With everyone dressed in dark clothing, they swept south on the Bisbee Road long after midnight. Crossing the Mule Mountains, they detoured around the copper-mining town, then trotted across the desert. Twice, they watered at tanks that Wyatt had located in earlier trips.

"His prospecting's been worth something after all," Doc said as he stood by his gelding drinking deep from a natural tank.

"Someday I'm going to find the damn mother lode too," Wyatt reminded him with a cold cigar in his mouth. He took it out. "And Gawdamn unbelievers like you ain't getting a damn penny out of it either."

"I'd hate to hold my breath until you find it."

"Mount up," Virgil said. "We can argue all day when this is over."

"Who's arguing, sah?" Doc asked, drawing himself up into the saddle.

"Not us," Wyatt said, and laughed aloud.

"Must be Slocum," Morgan Earp said, sharing a grin with him as the third Earp brother cradled a new Winchester in his arms and rode beside his stirrup.

"He's figuring how he can be twenty men again," Doc said over his shoulder.

"What's that?" Morgan asked softly.

"Oh, I busted up Ike's cow camp in Texas Canyon," Slocum said. "Doc said that Ike swore it took twenty men to do it."

"That's rich." Morgan slapped his knee and chuckled. "I heard you were a tiger when you got stormed up."

Slocum shrugged. Virgil wanted to lope some more, and raised his arm for them to follow him. As they set out, Slocum was grateful for the surefooted dun he'd taken from Curly Bill. The horse was tireless, besides being a cat on his feet. It had carried that elephant Curly Bill, so Slocum knew it would sure deliver him at half the big man's weight.

Close to dawn they reached the white tent beside the spring. The cottonwoods around the earthen tank rustled in the wind. Slaughter came outside with a cigar in his mouth, pants tucked in his boots, and a white shirt that almost glowed.

"Welcome to Rancho San Bernadino," he said as everyone dismounted and went to loosening cinches. The weary horses snored and blew as the black man began to gather them by the lead ropes.

"Watch that proud-cut bastard that Doc rides," Wyatt told the man.

"I done see him," the man said. "He sure be a rooster, I bet."

"Wyatt's jealous," Doc said. "He has to ride a stud to own one half as good as mine is."

Slocum waited until the others had gone to sit at the long table that Slaughter had set up outside the tent. Then he and Doc stepped away from the area and talked.

"Them two are sure keen on nailing your hide up," Doc said with a shake of his head. "I believe they went to Nogales, but they've been led astray before." He laughed to himself. "They got one goal in life, ain't they?"

"One goal in their mind, and they've been after it for a long time."

"Who pays them?"

"A rich man who lost his son in a gunfight."

"I understand. If it wasn't them, then he'd hire someone else, right?"

"Someone else who might be smarter than the Abbott brothers," Slocum said softly. "Thanks."

"I figured that out. If I wanted someone dogging me all the time, I'd want them a little slower than I was." The twinkle in his blue eyes sparkled at his discovery.

"Gentleman, breakfast is served," Slaughter announced to them from close by the tent entrance.

"Sah, I could eat an enormous portion too," Doc said, and they strode over for the meal.

The spread included fried eggs, ham, bread, peach jam, and gravy. The coffee was rich enough to wake Slocum up as he held the hot enamel cup in his hand and studied the others.

The Earp brothers could have been triplets. Shock-black hair, steel-blue eyes, long slender noses, broad shoulders, and all close to six feet tall. Without his hat, Doc's golden hair glistened in the sunlight as he talked and ate at the same time.

"We should be able to push to Arido by dark from here. Leave about noontime," Slaughter announced.

The nods of the bunch around the table were answer enough. No one acted disturbed, upset, or even anxious as far as Slocum could see. It was a job that needed doing and they were going to do it.

Had Carillo managed to get Ike and Finn there? What about Curly Bill and Ringo? This was different from an arrest. Only the winners would ride out.

They lounged around under the cottonwoods. Doc played solitaire and cheated. Slocum watched him with one eye, his back to the rough bark trunk. Morgan slept facedown on a blanket spread over the short grass. Wyatt paced like a caged lion and, all the time, whittled on spongy pieces of cottonwood branches with his huge jack-knife.

Later, Morgan and Slaughter played cribbage at the table. The morning passed slowly. Finally they saddled up, and then checked their firearms with lots of metallic clicking. In a few minutes, they started in a long trot into Mexico.

Slocum saw the white pillar left by the surveyors to mark the border. They were in Sonora and headed south. The only one who didn't need to know their destination was Old Man Clanton and his boys. Slocum hoped that was the case. He's been in on surprises before that had backfired and turned into traps.

Slaughter's man Bat led them close to the first range, and they skirted the base. Then they crossed more open country, and finally drew up in a dry wash. Slocum dismounted and drew a deep breath, loosening his girth and dropping the reins. The dun would ground-tie.

"We close?" Doc asked from the other side of his horse.

"Carillo should meet us here."

"If he's coming at all," Wyatt said. "I've had some dealings with them greasers. They ain't always so prompt or brave."

"This one is," Doc said. "He's a tough sum-bitch. You'll see."

"I wondered if this wasn't a trap to get us down here and then cut us down."

"Slocum, you tell Wyatt what you thought of our Mexican friend."

"He'd wanted to kill us, he'd do it himself," Slocum said, resting with his arms over the saddle.

"Must be tough," Wyatt declared.

"Tough enough," Doc said. "You'll see."

Carillo arrived with five armed men. Hollow-faced men with deep-set eyes to match the Earps. Bandoliers loaded with bullets crisscrossed their chests. The lines at the corners of their mouth were tight as fiddle strings, and each man rode a powerful horse equal to their boss's gray.

Pistoleros! Slocum recalled the song that Santa Anna's buglers had played at the Alamo. He had heard it a long ago in a Chihuahua cantina. The title in English was "*No Quarter Given.*"

"They played that song for Davy Crockett and Colonel Travis," the lusty doe-eyed whore in his lap had said. "All night they played it. Then at dawn . . ." She'd drawn the side of her hand knife-like across her throat. "No survivors."

"That damn Ike isn't at the ranch," Morgan muttered to Slocum, coming back from talking among the others. "Finn is in Charleston, they think, but he isn't coming. Curly Bill is going to miss the party, along with Ringo too."

"Did Carillo tell you all that?" Slocum asked.

"Yes, and he's mad."

"Nothing makes that man too happy anyway, the way I figure it," Slocum said, and mounted up.

"Old Man Clanton and a dozen cowboys are there."

"That's enough," Slocum said as he stood up in the stirrups to stretch his legs and then his stiff back while grasping the horn.

"Be a damn good start on cleaning the border up," Doc said, swinging his big horse around.

Plans were quickly made. Carillo and his men were to come from the west and close off the south. Morgan, Wyatt, and Doc were to ride in from the east. That left Virgil, Slaughter, and Slocum to take the front gate. Everyone nodded as the riders split off into the mesquite. Virgil held his big bay up with Slaughter on his black in the center of the two wagon tracks that wound southward through the dried brown foxtail. Slocum was on the right. Bat came behind them on a long-necked horse that showed its age. In the black man's arms was a long-barreled goose gun. Slocum decided it was either an eight- or ten-gauge.

"Let's ride, gents," Slaughter said, and they held their mounts to a steady walk. The animals sensed the impending confrontation. They bobbed their heads and acted impatient. Sometimes one of them shifted into a prance, moving sideways down the road only to be jerked back into a slower gait. Then one of the other mounts would break stride and dance on his forefeet.

"Horses know when something's up, don't they?" Virgil said, more a statement than a question.

"They do today. I've had horses shy and save my life too," Slaughter said.

"When you scout Apaches, you better believe your horse. He can see them before you ever will," Slocum added, noticing the low rambling adobe buildings ahead through the lacy mesquite foliage.

"That must be the old man's place," Slaughter said.

Slocum used his brass telescope to look it over. Someone had ridden up to the main house and was headed for the house.

"I think they just got warned," he said.

"By who?" Virgil demanded.

"I think an outrider. He ran to the front door."

"Damn!" Slaughter swore. "So much for surprises."

"Let's ride for it! The others had time to get in position!" Virgil said, and then he drew the Winchester out of the boot under his leg. "Rifles first!"

"Hee-yah!" The three men spread out as they raced through the flat desert around paloverdes and spreading mesquite. Someone appeared on the porch, and Virgil's rifle began to speak. Smoke poured out of the barrel, and his wide-eyed horse raced faster toward the building.

More puffs of gun smoke came from the ranch house. The range was too far; Slocum saved his bullets. Someone tore from the house and ran west toward the corrals. But in hail of gunshots he was stopped, and then he wilted in a pile.

"Carillo's men are in place," Slaughter shouted over the wind.

"Dismount," Virgil shouted, and they slid their horses to a stop.

The range was still too far. Slocum dismounted anyway and bellied down behind a small bank. He could hear someone swearing in the house. The rage of the man was like a wounded lion's roar.

"That's the old man," Virgil said as they took their places in line, an occasional bullet sending a shower of dust over them.

"Let's fill that house with bullets," Slaughter said. "I'll take the front door, Slocum, you take the right window, Virgil, the left ones, and fill them with all the bullets we have in our guns."

"Good idea." Virgil began to reload, lying on his side.

"Now!" Slaughter shouted, and they rose to shoot.

The three rifles barked as fast as the levers would work. In front of them, the ranch house exploded in a great ball of fire. Men's bodies were tossed hundreds of feet in the air, along with furniture, dust, and adobe.

Slocum, Virgil, and Slaughter blinked their eyes in disbelief at each other. Then they studied their rifles. Slocum shook his head. He swallowed hard as the shower of debris came down around them. Bits of wood and sticks from the roof rained on their hats.

"What the hell happened?" Slaughter asked.

"The damn explosives," Slocum said, recalling the store at the other ranch. "Clantons had a room full of explosives at the other ranch. I figure the old man had one here too and we hit it shooting at them."

"I'll be damned," Virgil said, beating the debris from his hat. "Ain't no one going to live in that fire it started either."

Slocum silently agreed as flames licked the sky two stories high. Old Man Clanton and his cowboys were no more. They probably never knew what hit them. The fire would save a funeral.

"You using new ammo?" Doc asked, riding over.

"Slocum said they stored lots of explosives at the other ranch and figured the old man did the same up here."

"Whew, it blew up big enough to take Wyatt's hat off and blow it to New Mexico." Doc shook his head, amused.

"Where is he?" Virgil asked with a frown.

"Chasing the hat he lost," Doc said, and then Carillo rode up.

"I figure Old Man Clanton has gone to roast in Hell," Doc said, holding his horn in both hands.

"Shame more of them didn't go with him," Carillo said, checking his excited gray. "But half of them are gone. *Amigos, gracia.*" He saluted them and turned the powerful horse on his hind feet. In a jump, the gray raced off through the mesquite and the man was gone.

"He never minced no words over him, now did he?" Slaughter said, amused, as he drew out a bottle of whiskey.

"I'd rather drink to him being in Hell than anything else," Doc said, drawing a tin cup from his saddlebags. "Time for an Irish wake, my friends, for Old Man Clanton."

Slocum drank one with them. Then he turned the dun horse southward. Maybe in the Sierra Madras, he could find a cool place. A pretty face to smile at him. No matter, it was time to move on.

Epilogue

November 1883

A cold wind swept off snowcapped Mount Graham. The force drove bitter grits of sand at Slocum's eyes and against his skin as he tucked his head under the hat. News of the OK Corral gunfight was over a year old. Old newspapers carrying the story of the shootout were yellowing in trunks. The Earps had left Tombstone. Morgan in a box, Virgil with his arm shattered. Slocum had already seen his partners at the Dragoon mine. Ferd and Monroe had counted out fifty ten-dollar gold eagles for his share. Probably more than what he deserved or what the mine had earned thus far. They had both been excited about a new shaft. The assay was better than the old one. He had shared some whiskey with them.

Had he heard that pretty Mrs. McClain was getting married? He had shaken his head. Yes, sir, to some engineer fellow, a mining man. Nice-looking too. Why, the whole town of Tombstone was taking a part in their wedding, to be held on New Year's Eve.

He reined up the bay horse. The leaves were gone from the cottonwoods around her place. Dust swirled around the yard before her front door as he considered whether to stop or not.

He tried to hear above the wind. Had he heard a shot? No, only the wind. He wouldn't know for a month that the blast that killed Ike Clanton had come that afternoon from a Wells Fargo guard's sawed-off shotgun during Ike's botched holdup attempt across the mountains. For a long time he sat on his mount, arguing with himself to stop or go on and doing neither.

Close to sundown, Slocum nudged the horse toward house. She came out and smiled at him.

"Been a long time," she said. Her eyes half squinted against the wind. She had to grasp her long hair to keep it from blowing. "I thought it was you sitting out there."

"It's been too long. I was passing through. I can ride on."

"No, don't do that."

"I guess he's at Wanda's, huh?"

"He stays up there. Put your horse up in the corral and come in. Bet you haven't ate, have you?"

"No, Naomia. I haven't ate." Maybe in a day or more. He couldn't recall when he'd eaten last.

She didn't trust him. He felt her watching him as he dismounted and lifted the stirrup up to undo the cinch. He tossed the saddle on the corral, then let the bars down and turned to smile at her.

"You can get out of the wind now, I'm coming," he said to reassure her.

"Good," she said, gathering her skirts and going inside.

The sun was sinking behind the bloody Dragoons. He turned his head, grasping his hat against the new blast. The interior of her house would be a safe haven from the eternal cold wind. Naomia's bed and charms would sooth him. He closed his eyes. *Mrs. McClain's marrying an engineer fella.*